SINKHOLE

A Horror Story

April A. Taylor

Cover designed by OliviaProDesign

This book is a work of fiction. Names, characters, places, and incidents either are products of the author's imagination or are used fictitiously. Any resemblance to actual persons, living or dead, events, or locales is entirely coincidental.

April A. Taylor
Visit my website at www.AprilATaylor.net

Printed in the United States of America

First Printing: October 2019
Midnight Grasshopper Books

ISBN: 978-1-69-721454-3

PREVIOUS WORKS

Corvo Hollows: A Psychological Thriller

The Haunting of Cabin Green: A Modern Gothic Horror Novel

Missing in Michigan: Alexa Bentley Paranormal Mysteries Book One

Frightened in France: Alexa Bentley Paranormal Mysteries Book Two

Lost in Louisiana: Alexa Bentley Paranormal Mysteries Book Three

Vasilisa the Terrible: A Baba Yaga Story (Midnight Myths and Fairy Tales #1)

Death Song of the Sea: A Celtic Story (Midnight Myths and Fairy Tales #2)

PRAISE FOR THE AUTHOR'S PREVIOUS WORKS

"Takes [the] standard genre template and turns it upside-down...the crazy whirlwind that ensues is enough to make even the biggest horror fan a bit dizzy...unique...with a literary approach that combines modern and mid-twentieth century techniques." - *Inquisitr, The Best Horror Books of 2018*

"Taylor weaves a haunting tale of a man who can't be sure if the desolate cabin he's staying in is full of ghosts or if his mind is playing tricks on him." - *Popsugar, The 13 Most Chilling Horror Books of 2018*

"I thought this would be a simple ghost story like *Paranormal Activity*. It wasn't. Filled with so much grief and craziness that I might need therapy." – *BoredPanda, 7 Horror Stories That Scared Me Half to Death*

"A spectacular read...absolutely gripping. I couldn't force myself to put it down. Taylor did an excellent and meticulous job creating this story, forming imagery...invoking real emotion on the part of the reader." - *The Horror Report*

"Unique... the author depicts the grieving process amazingly well. The story is claustrophobic... and what an ending. All of the flashbacks and delusions suddenly make sense... [it's a] sucker punch." - *HorrorTalk.com*

"Corvo Hollows is an edge of your seat thriller that grabs hold with the first line and doesn't let go even after the last page is turned. A must read!" - Reedsy Discovery

CONTENTS

This book is for everyone who loves horror.

PART ONE

Humanity

CHAPTER ONE

Southgate, MI

Allison gripped her toy truck as its wheels spun through the dirt. Despite her mother's attempts to the contrary, Allison's tomboy nature had punted all Barbies to the side. After their heads were removed, of course.

The eight-year-old girl with blonde pigtails envisioned a massive stretch of dirt where monster trucks battled for supremacy. In reality, her truck skidded around a tiny area in her family's suburban backyard.

The bird songs that served as her almost constant soundtrack stopped without warning, but Allison barely noticed. Content to live in a fantasy world, she continued to imagine the roar of the trucks.

The ground beneath her shook as her truck kicked into high gear. The squawking of birds returned in a cacophonous din just as an even louder crack split the earth open and sucked her inside. Allison grabbed a handful of grass as her screams filled the yard.

What in the world has she gotten into now? her mother, Carol, wondered. Dashing outside, Carol noted with dismay the agitated sounds of dozens of her beloved songbirds. *If she's done something to hurt one of them...*Her mouth dropped open as wide as the ground's maw that was greedily trying to gulp up her daughter in one bite.

"Allison!" she cried out. "Hold on!"

Allison's fearful, tear-streaked face poked slightly above the sinkhole that threatened to tear her mother's heart into tiny pieces. Carol noticed how feeble her daughter's grasp on the grass had become.

A burst of adrenaline propelled her forward with more speed than she would have thought possible from her aching, arthritic legs. Leaping like a baseball outfielder, she flew through the air and landed with an audible thud at the edge of the sinkhole.

Carol reached for Allison's hands just as her daughter's grip gave in to the downward force of gravity.

"I've got you! Hold on tight, baby girl," she said through gritted teeth. *My god, how much does she weigh?* Carol's muscles trembled as she fought against the enormous burden threatening to pull her and Allison deep into the earth.

"Mommy!" the girl yelped uncharacteristically. Allison had transitioned from saying 'Mommy' and 'Daddy' at such a young age that Carol's stomach lurched at the sudden reintroduction of the tender phrase.

Summoning her strength and courage, Carol yanked fiercely, no longer fearful of dislocating her daughter's shoulders. Anything would be better than giving into the demands of her tired muscles, which begged her to let go.

The two stumbled and Carol fell on her back. Allison held on tightly for a few seconds before scrambling over Carol's head.

"Come on," the girl urged her mother. "It's coming for us."

With that, Allison disappeared from view as she threw herself in the direction of the house.

What's coming for us?

With one last weary glance at the open pit – that seemed to be moving, somehow — Carol gathered enough strength to follow her daughter inside. The two soon sat next to each other on the couch as Allison recounted the experience from her point of view.

"I was playing with my truck, and the ground started shaking." A frown interrupted her story and tears filled her eyes. "Oh no...my truck. It's gone!"

Shocked by the anguished howl of Allison's last word, Carol reminded herself that children have a completely different set of priorities. She pulled her daughter closer and stroked her hair.

"We'll get you a new one, I promise."

Somewhat mollified, Allison continued, "I grabbed the grass, but something wrapped around my legs. I couldn't move."

"Wait, what do you mean something wrapped around your legs?"

"It grabbed me, Mommy. It wanted to pull me down. And it wanted you, too."

Allison's words were freaky, but Carol knew the young girl simply didn't have the right words to express what she'd experienced. To a child's mind, falling into a sinkhole probably felt very much like being literally pulled down by some type of unseen monster.

"You're okay," Carol tried to soothe away Allison's fears.

"No! I'm not! Stop saying that!"

Allison jumped off the couch and ran down the short hallway to her bedroom. Before Carol could intervene, Allison had slammed and locked the door.

"Allison?" Carol called gently while knocking. "Let me in, please."

"No," an impertinent voice responded. "You don't believe me," Allison sobbed.

"I'm sorry, baby girl."

Allison didn't reply. Sighing, Carol returned to the living room to give her daughter some time to deal with her fear. She flipped the TV on and got lost again within the crazy twists and turns of her favorite soap opera.

At the same time, Allison gingerly pulled off her blue jeans. Wicked rope burns scarred her alabaster flesh. She winced with her first exploratory touch.

See? I told you something grabbed me, she non-verbally pouted toward the closed door. "Parents never believe anything," Allison grumbled under her breath.

Later that day, her father, Scott, came home and became instantly enraged. "A sinkhole? You've got to be kidding me! It's that damn fracking, Carol. You know it is."

Carol nodded silently. She wasn't sure how fracking had anything to do with it, considering that they were three counties away from Michigan's closest hydraulic fracking site. Saying that to her angry husband was way too dangerous, so she kept her mouth shut – like usual.

"I'm taking this all the way to Lansing," he shouted while stabbing at buttons on his phone.

Sure. Like the governor is going to be sitting around, just waiting to take your call, she thought, irritated he hadn't shown more concern for their daughter.

As Carol predicted, Scott's call was passed on to a voicemail system. He ranted and raved about the hole in their backyard until the system unceremoniously cut him off, causing him to go off on a new tangent about his tax dollars entitling him to proper representation.

Unable to put up with his attitude any longer, Carol quietly left his side and wandered to the mailbox.

"What's Scott yelling about this time?" her nosy neighbor, Becky, asked. Becky's posture screamed annoyance, but her eyes sparkled in the hopes of getting some juicy gossip.

"A sinkhole opened up in the backyard."

"What?"

"A sinkhole. It came from out of nowhere and almost killed my kid."

"Oh my god, are you serious?" Becky took a few steps closer. Concern and intrigue duked it out for top billing on her face. Concern won out after a few seconds, but only by the slightest of margins. "Is she okay?"

Carol appraised her neighbor's new stance and expression. "Thanks for asking, Becky. It's a hell of a lot better than what her damn father did." She shot a sneering glare toward the backyard. "And yeah, she seems to be okay. Just scared, is all, but that's to be expected, right?"

"Absolutely," Becky concurred. "How did it happen?"

"I have no idea. Scott thinks it's fracking, but I don't know...Allison said something grabbed her and was pulling her into the ground, but that doesn't make much sense either, does it?"

"Hmmm...either way, it sure sounds odd."

Carol was pleasantly surprised by Becky's restraint. Normally, she would have taken a side and argued up a storm for it. This time, she seemed every bit as confused as Carol, which clearly sucked the wind out of her fiery sails.

"I know this is crazy...but...do you think it's possible something *was* trying to pull her in?"

Becky let Carol's question bounce through her mind for a few beats. It seemed preposterous, but so did a sinkhole appearing from out of nowhere.

"Well, I reckon that's the type of thing you'd have to ask an expert. But I've done a lot of digging and never seen anything like that. Unless she means the tree roots came to life," Becky laughed.

Carol usually bristled at Becky's insistence on talking like a southerner. The fifty-year-old woman had spent less than the first year of her life living in Texas, and yet she still peppered her speech with works like 'reckon.' Distracted by her own thoughts, Carol didn't react this time.

"Wait…what was that you said about tree roots?"

"That's the only thing I've ever seen while planting veggies. Never saw anything else when that terrible contractor dug up my yard, neither."

"Thanks, Becky," Carol's voice drifted as she made her way to the front door.

"No problem," Becky called out.

Carol slipped inside and went straight to the junk drawer. *Where is it?* she thought, flustered, as visions of evil tree roots slithered through her mind. Her fingers collided with a solid hunk of metal, and she pulled the flashlight free with a smile on her face.

Stalking with determination into the backyard, she straightened her back, puffed up her chest, and prepared for an argument with Scott. He was nowhere to be seen as she approached the sinkhole, but she knew he was probably already hitting the bottle hard and ready to spar.

Carol dropped to her knees and crept toward the edge. Her breath hitched in her throat as she peered over the edge. The flashlight came to life, but its strong beam failed to make much of an impact. She didn't see any monsters hiding in the ground, but something else jumpstarted her heart, making it race inside her chest.

The light was completely engulfed before she could spot the bottom of the hole. *Does it go all the way to Hell?* Unsure how to test her theory, Carol looked around until her eyes fell on one of her decorative rocks. They weren't too large for her to lift, but they certainly had enough heft to make an audible sound upon landing.

Here goes nothing.

She pitched the rock into the hole and waited. Several minutes later, when Scott stumbled into view from behind the garage, she still hadn't heard the rock hit anything. Carol scooted herself backward, certain that if she fell into the hole, she'd never stop falling.

CHAPTER TWO

Dunns, WV

Rachel and Ivy Meador stalked through the woods of southern West Virginia. The two sisters were mirror images physically, but they had little else in common except for a shared interest in genealogy. That familial bond had brought them to a town so small that only 200 people called it home.

Dunns was the type of place that had made *Little House on the Prairie* look like a modern story as recently as the 1960s. They knew some of their distant relatives lived in farmhouses during the '50s and '60s that hadn't been equipped with indoor plumbing. Some of those homes had even lacked electricity.

The twenty-three-year-old twins stood just over five feet. They had long, flowing brunette hair, sparkling green eyes, and slightly plump frames. Rachel's cheekbones were a hint fuller than Ivy's, but beyond that and Ivy's chipped tooth, it was practically impossible to tell the two apart. Until they opened their mouths, that is.

Hot sun beat down on them as they maneuvered between branches and fallen trees. The hunt for their great-grandmother's first home had taken them far off the main dirt road, which shared its name with the town. It was common to find abandoned structures dotted throughout the wilderness, and the instructions they'd been given made it clear that hiking was the sole way to reach their destination.

Sweat-soaked long pants and thin, long-sleeved shirts made the women miserable. But the fear of being bitten by a tick was engrained far too deeply into Ivy's psyche for either of them to dress in a seasonably appropriate manner.

Rachel silently cursed Ivy's nervousness.

This is ridiculous. I could be wearing comfy clothing, but little Ms. Paranoia strikes again.

An old wooden farmhouse caught their attention in the distance.

"I bet that's it!" Ivy said.

"It'd better be," Rachel grumbled. She was every bit as responsible as Ivy for having planned this trip. Now that they were here, though, her interest in genealogy had taken a backseat to her love for modern conveniences – especially air conditioning.

Ivy pulled out a camera and started lovingly documenting everything. She issued a series of "oohs" and "aahs" as she got her first good look at the dilapidated property through a zoom lens.

With the house finally in sight, Rachel started warming back up to the entire purpose of their trip. And she had to admit that the old structure seemed to magically transport her back in time.

A few yellowed and weather-beaten 'No Trespassing' signs were tacked to the surrounding trees. Ignoring them, Ivy and Rachel craned their necks upward as they took in the surprisingly well-constructed home.

Made solely from wood and nails – at least as far as they could tell – there were two sections to the house. The front portion held the living room and had a seven-foot-high ceiling. The back expanded to two stories, and they knew before walking inside there'd be a loft area for sleeping. The similarities to *Little House on the Prairie* apparently went even further than either of them had expected.

As they stepped closer to the house, a whisper floated through the trees.

"What was that?" Ivy asked.

"What was what?" Rachel responded.

"Didn't you say something?"

"No."

Confused, they took a couple more steps before halting.

"There! Hear that?" Ivy said.

Rachel nodded. She had no idea who – or what – was making the noise, but it almost sounded like the trees themselves were trying to speak. Shaking off that idea as nonsensical, the twin sisters stepped forward again.

A brown blur raced through the corner of Rachel's vision. She went airborne before she could react and landed with a hard thump. She released a painful scream as an intrusive presence chomped down on her arm. Rachel struggled to face her opponent, and her mouth fell open.

What the fuck?

A tawny-colored deer with a white belly and white spots had pinned her to the ground. Blood dripped free of its otherwise adorable face. Momentarily paralyzed, Rachel couldn't decide what to do, and this hesitation allowed the deer to rip through her flesh again.

Ivy tried to distract the deer by yelling and tossing sticks and rocks at it, but her actions had zero effect. The deer stuck with its meal like a dog with a juicy steak. Horrified, Ivy ripped her phone free of her purse, only to be met with the inevitable: no signal.

"Help! Help us, please!" Ivy shouted as her sister screamed again, although she knew in her gut no one was around for miles.

What do I do? Ivy thought frantically as the seemingly rabid deer continued to ignore her efforts.

The air was ripped in half by the startling sound of a gunshot. The deer reared back on its hind legs, whining in agony and licking its lips. A heartbeat later, it fell backward, and Ivy gratefully noted that it'd missed crushing her sister by less than an inch.

Ivy dropped to her knees, ripping the bottom edge free of her shirt. "Are you okay?" she said while hastily wrapping her sister's wounds.

"What the fuck just happened?" Rachel mumbled.

Ivy had to suppress a laugh. If Rachel was issuing her characteristic swearing, things couldn't be that bad, right?

Just as Ivy started convincing herself that her sister was going to be okay, she noticed that beads of sweat were rapidly dotting Rachel's forehead. Rachel's normally pale skin had also turned a deep shade of red, and her eyes took on the hazy glow of cataracts.

"Looks like you could use a hand?" a deep but friendly voice said with a questioning lilt.

Ivy turned around in time to spot the arrival of a tall, solidly built man with a rifle strap slung over his shoulder.

"That was you? Thank you so much," Ivy said in a rush of jumbled words.

"No problem," the man smiled before drawing closer to Rachel's prone form. Her body trembled with muscle spasms, although she seemed unconscious otherwise.

"Shit!" he said. "You need a hospital. Let's go!"

The man tossed aside his rifle and picked Rachel up as if she weighed less than a kitten. He hurried toward the main road. Ivy struggled to keep up.

"Should we call 911?" she asked.

"No time," he replied. "We're at least half-an-hour from the closest hospital. If we wait for an ambulance to get here..."

"Half-an-hour?" she shrieked in fear. "What about a doctor? Surely, there's someone closer?"

"Yeah, by about five minutes, maybe. Trust me, the hospital is your best bet."

Uncertain what to think, Ivy allowed the stranger to place her sister inside the extended cab of his truck.

"Hop in," he urged her, and she complied.

He took off, leaving a cloud of dust in the truck's wake. Ivy's knuckles turned white as she held on. If Rachel had been her normal self, she would have already cracked a joke about Ivy clutching the "oh shit!" handle. A tear raced down her cheek as Ivy wondered if she'd ever hear that joke again.

Hang on, sister.

CHAPTER THREE

Centralia, PA

An empty fast food wrapper blew into Don's yard. Infuriated, he barked to himself about the "damn tourists" who kept "mucking up" his town. When he was born, the small mining town had more than two-thousand residents. But now, after the disastrous underground coal fire and decades of neglect, he was one of only a handful of people left.

That didn't mean the virtual ghost town's streets stood empty. Far to the contrary, in fact, ever since that *Silent Hill* movie came out in 2006. There was something about the combination of a human-made disaster and the aptly named Graffiti Highway that kept gawkers and lovers of ruin porn coming around.

Never mind how disrespectful it is or how many warning signs we put up, Don thought. *Someone's going to get themselves killed one of these days, mark my words.*

Don had been airing these sentiments to anyone who would listen for years. Most people shook their heads and asked why he didn't move away from Centralia if it was so dangerous. But he'd be damned if he'd take a government payout that wasn't worth even half of the value of the home his great-grandfather had built with his own two hands. And besides, he reasoned, at the age of seventy-nine, he probably didn't have much time left anyway.

Don was the only resident in town who had a functional vehicle. The Sabinskis also owned a car, but it had broken down last week. Getting that towed to a repair shop would cost a pretty penny, and the Sabinskis hadn't done so yet.

Serves them right for buying foreign crap, Don had thought when they'd told him. He didn't realize that the South Korean brand was assembled by American workers in Georgia, nor would that have shaken his long-standing commitment to buying Ford trucks.

Don covered his gray hair with a red baseball cap he'd left on his favorite lawn chair. His eyes peered around the neighborhood, seeing nothing but emptiness. The skinny, tall house he'd inherited from his parents was the only sign of civilization left on the block. Everyone else had sold out, and the government had leveled their properties.

Sure, the occasional concrete steps to nowhere existed, along with a few crumbling foundations. He also stood only a block away from the Sabinski house, along with an old, dilapidated brick wall that looky-loos had graffitied to Hell and back. But if it hadn't been for his dedication to giving his riding lawnmower a good workout once a week, every abandoned yard near his would have become a wild, tangled mess.

The rumble of a vehicle on Locust Avenue pulled his thoughts out of the past. "Keep going, keep going," he whispered, but to no avail. As expected, another group of adventure-seekers had stopped off the main road, near the cemetery. Don got into his big Ford pickup truck, checked the shotgun on the inside gun rack, and drove off with his blood boiling.

Not this time, fuckers.

Less than a week ago, a few teenagers had trashed the cemetery by breaking empty liquor bottles on several headstones. He'd pledged then and there that the next idiot to trespass in his town would end up with some buckshot stuck in their ass.

As expected, a car sat parked in front of the cemetery. He didn't see anyone walking through the headstones, which could only mean one thing; they'd trekked over to the hidden Graffiti Highway.

Goddammit.

Hiking down the old main highway wasn't a problem, but getting back up could be horrific, especially on a hot day like today. The steep slope was rough enough on its own. Even worse, the noxious fumes from the underground fire that had been burning since 1962 were very prevalent in this area of town.

He stood pondering his options at the shabbily covered entrance to Graffiti Highway when a sharp cry for help made his legs start moving. *Now someone's done it.*

Don couldn't see the screamer yet, but he was fairly certain it was a young man. *If he's not dying, I'm going to kill him.*

Don's wrinkled skin seemed even drier than usual as the fumes reached out to encircle his head. Red blotches broke out across his cheeks and forehead. He clutched his shotgun tightly as he rounded a slight curve in the road. A blast of unimaginable heat hit him in the face and chest. Don stumbled backward and fell on his ass.

That's going to hurt in the morning, he mentally moaned as he picked himself back up off the ground. The screaming returned with the intensity of someone being chased by an axe murderer.

I'm coming, I'm coming. Hold your damn horses.

Flames shot into the sky, licking the clouds and suffocating the air. "What the Sam Hell?" he shouted, not caring that he'd just butchered an old phrase.

Tears ran down the sides of his face as smoke and soot filled his eyes. He removed the handkerchief from his pocket and hastily covered his mouth and nose. Every nerve ending in his body urged him to run back the way he'd come, but he couldn't bring himself to leave without finding the source of the screams.

Edging closer to the graffiti-covered road's main fissure – the one popularized by *Silent Hill* – his trembling hands fell to his side. The once useful handkerchief turned black from soot before it landed on top of the spray-painted words "Shhh...I'm a dinosaur."

During previous visits, Don had always expressed his disdain at the weird things people chose to write on the decommissioned highway. This time, he didn't see anything except for the living nightmare approximately ten-feet away.

Screams echoed louder and louder throughout the otherwise vacant landscape, accompanied by the crackling sound of fire eating its way through human flesh. The acrid odor broke through Don's stupor, bringing his partially digested lunch with it.

Too disturbed to even notice the vomit on his shoes, Don struggled to reach the right decision. Should he simply bail before the same thing happened to him? Or could the man be saved? And if not, wouldn't it be more humane to put him out of his misery?

No one could live through that.

His hands shook again as he pulled the shotgun into position against his right shoulder. The shrieking inferno flailed more wildly than before, as if the man inside of it understood Don's plan and didn't approve.

"I'm sorry," Don said. "Forgive me."

A bullet flew from the tip of the shotgun, temporarily separating the smoke before becoming lost in the haze. A second later, the wailing of the fire's victim came to an abrupt end.

Shell shocked, Don struggled to remain upright. The fire had seen him, and he intuitively understood that if he fell, he would never get back up. He ran. Despite his hip pain, despite his tortured, smoke-filled lungs, despite every ache and pain that marked his age, he ran faster than he had since his 20s.

Flames kissed his back, and Don's legs somehow pumped even harder. Fifty yards from safety, a terrifying cracking sound caused him to look back. Graffiti Highway's many small cracks and fissures were widening by the second. Fire shot through each opening.

Don was convinced the flames were sentient and had only one goal in mind: killing him for his interference. Only this time, there would be no bystanders to put him out of his misery.

Ten more yards to go. *You can do this,* he urged himself. Five. Four. Three. His feet stumbled on a newly opened crack, sending his body airborne. The last yard of the blacktop opened wide, and flames singed the back of his hair as he flew overhead.

Don landed a mere yard outside of the fire's reach. It roared in displeasure, and he could have sworn there were words inside of its rage. Grateful for the tall, unkempt grass that broke his fall – but unwilling to trust it any further – Don stood up with plans to run again. An involuntary scream ripped free of his lips as every bone in his right foot demanded relief.

Shit!

His truck stood a mere fifty-feet away, but the distance seemed insurmountable. Looking around wildly for something, anything that could help, he found a solid-looking stick.

This'll have to do.

Bracing his bruised and battered body for the next ordeal, Don leaned on the stick and used it to hop one-footed to his truck. He jammed the stick down on the gas pedal. As he peeled out of the parking spot, his mind raced with the implications of everything he'd just witnessed. The flames had never been that bad even back during the fire's heyday. What the hell was going on?

CHAPTER FOUR

Southgate, MI

Carol's skin reflected the blueish hue of the old television in the dimly lit living room. She'd become transfixed by local and cable news during the past twenty-four hours.

"Reports of sinkholes continue to pour in from across the state of Michigan. No one has been able to determine exactly what's causing these disturbing occurrences, but one thing seems clear. If you're outside, especially in a grassy area, it's critical to stay alert for any odd sounds or movements. Most of the witnesses we've spoken to say the ground trembled like an earthquake before it cracked open."

The camera panned into a sinkhole. Even with professional lighting, the end of the hole wasn't visible.

"As you can see, these sinkholes go very far into the ground. Be sure to contact local authorities if one appears near you, and keep all children and pets far away from them. So far, at least one death has been blamed on these odd disturbances. Reporting live from Royal Oak, I'm Diane Douglas for Channel 7 News."

Scott stumbled into the living room, drunk as a skunk and ready to fight, like always. "Why the hell are you watching that? It's nothing but depressing garbage."

"There've been sinkholes popping up all over the state, Scott. Something really weird is happening."

"Like I said, it's that damn fracking. Gonna kill us all," he slurred.

"Do you think we should go somewhere else for a while?"

"Like where? Unless you won the lottery and didn't tell me, we ain't got enough money to go nowhere."

We might if you didn't drink your paycheck away, Carol thought. She wanted so badly to express her thoughts, but Scott's voice had already risen to a dangerously high volume. If he became more agitated, an argument would break out for sure.

"You're right," she conceded.

"Damn right, I am! That's the smartest thing you've said all day."

I wish you'd fallen into that hole, you bastard.

"I'm going to take Allison out to play," Carol said, looking for any excuse to get away from her husband.

"The hell you are," he barked. "You're the one sitting there telling me that sinkholes are all over the state. Why would I let you take my daughter outside? You trying to get her killed?"

Scott pressed his face against Carol's. The alcoholic fumes wafting out of his slightly open mouth were almost enough to get her buzzed by proxy. She knew this was an intimidation technique, and she wasn't going to give him the satisfaction of getting physical.

"You're right," she whispered. "We'll play in her room."

Satisfied, Scott sat down on the couch and flipped to the Detroit Tigers game as Carol slinked down the hallway.

Dumbass, Scott thought before the crack of the bat made him forget all about his wife. He cracked open a new beer, and some of the dark brown liquid shot out onto the floor. If he'd been sober, he might have tried to clean up the mess. Instead, he chose to ignore it in favor of eating a handful of potato chips.

The Tigers took the field against the Minnesota Twins. After the last half-inning, the team sporting white uniforms emblazoned with the old English D was up by one run.

The cleanup hitter for the Twins stepped up to the plate with a bleach blond Louisville Slugger and the cocky expression of someone who was having a great season. The pitcher battled the opposing team's top hitter to a full count but made a mistake after serving up four fly balls in a row.

"Dammit!" Scott shouted as the ball left the bat. He just knew it was going to get past the infielders and would be worth at least a single, if not a double.

The nimble Detroit shortstop leaped to intercept the ball. Against all odds, he snagged the white bullet out of the air. He turned his body toward first base while still elevated above the infield dirt, confident that his landing foot placement would be perfect as always, along with his throw.

A rumble filled the stadium as fans roared. This quickly turned into a hushed silence as the infielder's feet hit the dirt. He instinctually threw the ball to first while his feet were sucked into the ground. The first baseman made a highlight reel worthy catch and tagged the runner as his teammate disappeared.

"What the...? Holy shit!" Scott sat in stunned silence for a moment after his outburst.

The rest of the Tigers and most of the Twins crowded over to the new sinkhole to see if they could help their fallen comrade. It soon became clear the athlete had been sucked in before he could grab onto anything. The shortstop's pleas for help lasted much longer than Scott thought possible, but that wasn't the worst part. No, it got much worse when the man's screams faded out of range of the stadium's camera and audio system.

"Carol! Get your ass in here!"

Normally, she tried to avoid responding to his drunken summons. But something about Scott's voice told Carol this wasn't going to be about any of his typical foolishness.

She rushed into the living room just as a replay of the shortstop's impressive play took over the screen.

"What is it?"

"Shhh. Watch, dammit!"

Carol enjoyed baseball but was a bit perturbed at being interrupted for a replay. Her mood quickly turned to abject horror as the earth swallowed her favorite player. Absurdly, her first thought was *who's going to be my Tiger now?* in response to the long-running "Who's Your Tiger?" marketing campaign.

Scott turned to her, sobered by what he'd seen, and asked, "Did that really just happen?"

"Yeah," she uttered in shock.

They'd been together since high school and had gotten married at the age of eighteen. Twenty years later, there were days when she could swear she didn't even recognize him anymore. She'd contemplated divorce on several occasions, even going so far as to speak to a lawyer once.

But in that moment, the fragile innocence that entered his eyes and words almost broke her heart. "I'm scared, Carol," he trembled.

"I am, too, sweetie. I am, too."

She stood in front of his sitting form and allowed his arms to encircle her waist like they did before alcohol and anger came between them. Her hands caressed his hair, and they both wondered if they were facing the end of days.

CHAPTER FIVE

Princeton, WV

Thaddeus expertly drove his truck as the woman in the back cab moaned in and out of consciousness. He'd tossed the green John Deere cap off of his head during the tense ride and now pushed his thick black hair back repeatedly. He risked another sidelong glance at the bleeding woman's sister before returning his eyes to the road.

"My name's Thaddeus, by the way."

Ivy's thoughts were so thick they'd sucked her in like a pool of molasses. It took a few seconds for her to realize the man had spoken, and when she did, she had no recollection of what he'd just said.

"I'm sorry. What was that?"

"My name's Thaddeus."

Silence.

Nervous, he pushed his hair back yet again and said, "I know, it's a weird name, right? You can call me Thad instead. Or Tad. Either works."

Distracted, she finally responded. "Okay, Thad. I'm Ivy. That's my sister, Rachel," she motioned toward the cab.

"Sisters? Really? I wouldn't have guessed," he responded with a hint of jocularity in his voice.

Ivy missed his attempt at humor. "Yeah, sisters. Twins, actually."

"So I gathered," he said quietly. "We'll be there in a couple of minutes, Ivy. I'm sure your sister is going to be okay." But he wasn't sure. Rachel's pallor had grown paler by the minute, and he knew the long drive to the big city had been detrimental for her.

If only someone would open an urgent care or even just a doctor's office closer to Dunns, dammit.

In truth, the trip from Dunns to Princeton usually took closer to thirty-five minutes than half-an-hour, but he hadn't wanted to stress Ivy out even more. On the plus side, he'd managed to cut seven minutes off that time by speeding. They turned right onto 12th Street and slid smoothly into Princeton Community Hospital's parking lot.

The light tan and brown bricks caught Ivy's attention as Thad parked next to the small emergency room entrance. The building was much shorter than the hospital she was used to, but the overall campus spread out farther than expected.

Thad pulled Rachel out with as much gentleness as he could muster while still rushing. Ivy jogged to match his pace, and they soon found themselves approaching the desk.

"Please help me! My sister was attacked by a wild deer."

"I'm sorry, what?" said the incredulous looking woman behind the counter.

"A deer bit her. Twice! Looked kind of rabid."

The woman lowered her reading glasses and gave Ivy a skeptical glance before turning her attention to the incoming patient. Rachel hung limply in Thad's arms. Her ghostly pale face and continuously bleeding arm snapped the woman into high gear.

A moment later, two male nurses wheeled a trauma stretcher into the waiting room. "Put her down here," one of them barked at Thad. Before Ivy could even think of anything to say or ask, the men had wheeled her sister away.

Reeling from everything that had happened, Ivy sat down hard on a green-cushioned chair. Tears flowed freely as worry wormed its way through her mind, heart, and stomach.

A sense of ineffectiveness washed over Thad. He didn't know either of these women but had taken on some responsibility for their well-being. Unsure how to console Ivy, he walked to the corner coffee machine and bought her a cup.

"I got this for you."

Ivy's terror-stricken eyes met his, and Thad knew she was torturing herself with worst-case scenarios.

"Take a sip. It might help," he said, feeling lame but uncertain what other platitudes to offer.

A nurse dressed in red scrubs burst out of the emergency room and called out, "Ms. Meador?"

Ivy jumped out of her seat and raised her hand.

"Can you tell me what happened to Rachel?"

"She was attacked by a deer. It bit her twice."

"Did you notice anything unusual about the animal?"

"Other than the fact that it slammed my sister to the ground and started eating her arm, you mean?" Ivy snapped with a sarcastic tenacity that only Rachel could muster during normal circumstances.

"Was it foaming at the mouth, drooling, maybe breathing hard?"

Ivy took a beat to shift through her memories of the attack. She also turned to Thad. "I didn't see anything like that. What about you?"

"I don't know. I mean, my first thought was rabies, but come to think of it...no, I didn't notice anything like that. It seemed more dazed, almost as if it was surprised it could even pull off running and biting like that."

The nurse jotted down a few notes. "Where is the deer now?"

"I put it down," Thad said. "So, it should be there in the woods still. Back in Dunns. Say...you don't think it's that zombie deer disease they've been talking about on the news, do you?"

"Zombie de...oh, you must mean chronic wasting disease? It's possible, I suppose...did it seem thin for a deer?"

"Come to think of it, yeah, it did," he responded.

"It would certainly match the aggressive tendencies of CWD...I tell you what, I'll go run that by the doctor."

"When can I see her?" Ivy asked.

"Sit tight, for now. I'll let you know when it's okay for you to go back there."

Ivy slumped down into the chair and took a half-hearted sip of coffee.

"They're going to take care of her. And I'm going to stay right here until they do. Deal?" Thad said.

Gratitude welled up inside of Ivy as she considered Thad's words and actions. She'd met him less than an hour ago, but he was currently the second most important person in her world. After all, Rachel would probably have died without his help.

"Deal," she said while lightly touching his arm.

CHAPTER SIX

Centralia, PA

Don's truck came to a halt outside a nicely maintained home owned by Jill and Doreen Sabinski. The two had lived in Centralia since the 1970s, and they'd initially introduced themselves to their new neighbors as sisters. Don had long had his doubts about that claim. But even now, long after public sentiment had turned in ways that boiled his blood, the two women held on to their story.

He spoke to them a couple of times per week, despite his discomfort with what he assumed to be their true lifestyle. And in a moment like this, there was truly no one else for him to turn to. Frustrated and in pain, he laid on his truck's horn for a few seconds to get their attention.

Doreen stuck her head outside and said, "Good lord, Don. You almost gave me a heart attack! What's going on?"

"Get Jill, would you? I think I broke my foot," he responded as rivulets of sweat poured down his face.

Doreen dashed inside and found her wife – legally since 2017, and in her heart since the late 1960s – exiting the bathroom. "Don's out front. Said he broke his foot? His face is about as red as that hat of his," she chuckled.

Jill shook her head and clucked her tongue. "Ugh. I'll get my medical bag."

When they'd first moved to Centralia, they knew it was against their best interests to reveal the true nature of their relationship. After so many years, it seemed pointless to change their public persona now.

They saw the way Don looked at them, though. They knew he'd figured it out, but they'd be damned if they'd confirm his suspicions. Both women were in their 70s, enjoying their retirement and living mortgage free. They weren't going to let anything chase them off.

Jill approached the truck and heard Don wincing.

"Hurry up, would ya?" he said with more than a hint of irritation.

"You know, Don, most people would be a lot nicer after asking for free healthcare."

He rolled his eyes. "I thought that's what people like you wanted for the entire country."

Unwilling to get sucked into a political debate, she changed course by saying, "Stretch out lengthwise across the seat so I can take a look."

See, Martha? The bench seat did come in handy, he mentally chided his deceased wife.

Jill untied his shoe and removed it to a chorus of groans and negative chatter, all of which she ignored. Getting the cantankerous man's sock off was even trickier, but she'd dealt with much worse during her forty-year career as a nurse.

She poked and prodded at his foot – perhaps a smidge more roughly than was strictly necessary – before asking him to try to move it in a few different directions. "It's hard to say for sure without an x-ray, but it looks like you've probably got a hairline fracture. That's the good news. The bad news is you're going to have to stay off your feet for a while."

She wrapped his foot in an ace bandage and said, "You should ice that at least a couple of times per day. Take some acetaminophen, too. Oh, and if you still have those crutches, be sure to use them."

Don grimaced at the mention of Martha's crutches. Jill's empathetic side took over, ignoring all the nasty looks she and Doreen had received from him over the years. "I'm sorry, Don," she said.

"It's nothing," he muttered, unwilling to be comforted by his neighbor.

"Anything else going on? I could have sworn I heard a gunshot earlier."

His eyes drifted from her face. He debated the pros and cons of telling her before offering only a partial truth. "I heard it, too. Damn looky-loos. I went to check on it but didn't find anyone. The fissure's acting up something awful, though."

Her eyebrows furrowed. "What do you mean?"

"Well, when was the last time you saw any fire coming out of it?"

"It's got to be what, twenty or thirty years ago, now?"

"That's what I thought, too, but try telling that to the fissure. Damn thing's spitting out flames today and breaking up even more. Craziest thing I ever saw."

"Flames? What kind of flames?"

He looked at her like she'd lost her mind. "What the hell do you mean what kind of flames? They were *flame* flames. Big ones, too."

"Do you think we should be worried?"

"What? No. Been here my whole life, and I ain't leaving on account of some stupid flames and new cracks on the old highway. Besides, we're safe here."

"Fair enough," she nodded. "You're all patched up for now, then. Take it easy, and...just promise you'll let me know if anything else odd happens, okay?"

"Sure enough, but I can't imagine what that would be."

And I don't want to imagine it, she thought.

CHAPTER SEVEN

Southgate, MI

Carol shot a sideways glance toward her husband. She'd been praying for him to stop drinking since his disillusionment drove him to the bottle in late 2016. But now that he'd actually spent twenty-four hours sober, she didn't know how to deal with his emotional fragility.

Scott's face rested inside his palms as tears created a shallow pond. Visions of alcohol teased him with the promise of liquor's cold embrace. It had allowed him to block out the rest of the world at a time when he felt depression knocking on his door. But he understood that he needed the solid warmth of sobriety right now, even if it threatened to send him spiraling downward.

"Carol?" he said weakly, testing the distance that had grown between them.

"Yes?"

"I'm sorry."

"For what?"

"For all of it. Everything. For who I've become," he sobbed.

She'd enjoyed their rare embrace the day before but was uncertain if she could actually forgive him for his many, many trespasses upon her heart and body. Rather than say something that could sully the moment, she opted to go mute.

"It's okay if you hate me. I hate me," he said. "But I promise to be better." His bleary, blood-shot eyes sought her out as he lifted his head. Their gazes locked for a faltering second before he turned away in shame.

If I'd known that seeing a hole open up and swallow a person would have the power to change him... she mused.

Two days ago, she'd listened to him babble on and on about government conspiracies and stolen political seats. He'd long ago become just as bad – if not worse – than the people he viewed as his enemies.

"Come on, sweetie," she offered in a conciliatory tone.

He looked up again and gratefully accepted the box of tissues from her hand. With a loud honking sound that rivaled a flock of Canadian geese, he rid himself of some of the heaviness he'd held inside.

"We should check on Allison," he said after drying his cheeks.

He started to knock on his daughter's door but hesitated. Sensing his reluctance, Carol reached past him and pushed the door open. She saw nothing but a massive sinkhole, and her heart beat triple time.

"Allison?" Carol called out before pinching her eyes shut.

"Yeah?" her daughter replied.

Relief flooded her body as her newly opened eyes drank in the room. Everything was normal, including the messy floor. Allison's drawing on her plastic easel was less than inspiring, though. It featured a gaping hole in the ground that resembled a mouth. Tentacles protruded from the surface, grabbing onto the decorative rocks and lawn décor from their backyard.

Carol had to swallow the urge to condemn the art. It terrified her, but she knew enough about child psychology to recognize it as a coping mechanism. Allison had fallen into that hole, after all; not her or Scott. And she needed to process it in her own way.

Scott didn't come to the same conclusion. He avoided the maze of monster trucks, LEGOs, and other toys before lowering himself to his haunches at Allison's side.

He pointed at the tentacles in the young girl's art and asked, "What are those?"

"The monsters," she responded firmly.

"Monsters?"

"Yes, the monsters that grabbed me."

Scott's face slackened and Carol's mind jumped to judging him. *How could he believe such nonsense?*

"That's how she's coping with it, Scott."

"Are you sure?" he asked.

"Of course. That's what all the books say."

Allison stomped on the ground and yelled, "They're real!"

"Honey, you know that's not true, right? There's no such thing as monsters."

"I can prove it!" Allison roared with her high-pitched, angry voice.

"Okay, honey. I'm listening," Carol said with as much patience and tolerance as she could muster.

Allison started to peel off her sweatpants.

"Whoa, what are you doing there?" Scott said as he turned around. He knew she was his daughter, and only eight, but he still felt distinctly uncomfortable. It seemed wrong, somehow, like an invasion of the privacy she didn't know she should expect.

A harsh intake of air caused him to spin back around.

"Oh my god, what is that?" Carol cried and dropped to her knees.

"Told ya," Allison said with a satisfied tone.

Carol reached out to touch the markings on Allison's legs before halting abruptly. "Do they hurt?"

Allison shrugged.

Carol allowed herself to lightly touch one of the dark lines. Allison winced, and Carol immediately stopped investigating the wounds.

"How did this happen?" Scott demanded.

"I told you already. It was the monsters," Allison pouted.

Rage swarmed around Scott's head.

"Did you do this to her?" he asked Carol. "Trying to prove a point or something? I *know* I've been a terrible father. You don't have to rub it in, dammit!"

"What the hell are you talking about? I didn't do this," Carol screeched. "And to think that I thought you might change. Hah," she spat.

Scott stormed out of the room. Allison sniffled, catching her mom's attention.

"Why is Dad mad at me?"

"He's not, baby girl. He's mad at himself," Carol said and hoped it was the truth.

CHAPTER EIGHT

Princeton, WV

Thaddeus was a man of his word, but he'd also grown extremely tired during the prolonged wait. His eyes slipped shut and jerked open several times before a wave of exhaustion claimed him.

Ivy took in his sleeping form and almost smiled. He was a tall man with more than enough strength to carry her sister, yet his face had become as innocent as a young child's. *Sleep well,* she thought and actually meant it.

Without Thad's company to keep her mind engaged, she started gnawing over one catastrophizing thought after another. Would her sister survive? And if she did, would she be too sick to go home? Their mom had been opposed to the trip – would she hold Rachel's injuries against her?

Ivy didn't understand her mom's reluctance. This was her side of the family, after all, and the twins had thought she'd be thrilled to tell them all about it. Instead, she'd made vague comments about leaving the dead alone before cutting off the conversation altogether. When Ivy and Rachel told her about their upcoming trip, she'd advised them against it, but wouldn't explain herself any further.

Come to think of it, their mom had never told them much about her own immediate family, let alone the extended version that hailed from Dunns and other parts of West Virginia. They'd always written it off as her simply having a lack of interest in genealogy. But now, her evasiveness seemed almost sinister. Had she known something like this might happen?

CHAPTER NINE

Centralia, PA

Don sat motionless in front of the TV. His favorite news pundit raged against every other news channel for misinforming its viewers. The vitriolic commentary behind the man's words had long had a welcoming home within Don's mind.

Half-listening, Don's thoughts drifted to the man he'd shot. It had clearly been a mercy killing. No sane jury on earth would convict him of a crime. There were much more important questions to focus on now such as who the man was and what the hell had happened?

Don had always believed Centralia wasn't a place for outsiders and had recently sworn to protect it. Now his thoughts seemed almost prophetic. He became adamant that any further contamination from the outside world would only anger the fire even more. He likened it to a plague.

This is God's wrath, and I'm his instrument.

The corners of Don's mouth curved upward as he daydreamed about protecting the small town with his shotgun and a shovel.

Next time, I won't hesitate.

♦ ♦ ♦

Jill and Doreen had debated the pros and cons of checking on Don's claim, but in the end, Jill's curiosity had won.

"What the..." Doreen uttered as they took in the utter destruction of Graffiti Highway.

"I don't see any flames. Do you?" Jill asked.

Doreen squinted her eyes and peered as far down the highway as she could. "No, but you know we can't see past the curve. It sure does smells like smoke, though."

"Yeah," Jill responded uncomfortably. "And a few other things, too."

Doreen took a deep sniff and recoiled. "What *is* that?"

"I've only smelled it a few times before...at the hospital," Jill said.

"And?"

Jill took her wife's hand. "It's burnt flesh. Human flesh."

"Oh, my lord," Doreen responded. "Do you think...I mean, what the heck was Don doing out here, anyway?"

Echoing her earlier sentiment, Jill said, "I'm not sure I want to know."

"Do you think we're in danger?"

"What, from Don? Nah. He can't even stand up straight on his own. Whatever happened here bit him back really good, I'd say."

"Probably deserved it," Doreen observed.

"Too bad the fire didn't eat that ugly hat of his," Jill laughed bitterly.

CHAPTER TEN

Southgate, MI

The sting of anger erupted from Scott's knuckles as they repeatedly bit into an old punching bag. Sweat dripped down his face and back as he tried to remember when he'd last been sober enough to make the bag buck with such a satisfying pop.

He'd been a fairly good boxer during his late-teens and had even briefly entertained the notion of boxing professionally. Getting past the amateur ranks would have taken a miracle, but he still would have tried if there'd been enough money in it for even a meager existence.

His love for Carol had stopped him from putting his body – and financial stability – on the line. Even though he knew this had probably saved him from a very painful and short-lived career, he still allowed himself to hold it against her from time-to-time. In moments like this one, it was simply easier to blame all of his woes on her than on himself.

Have a drink, his inner demons whispered beguilingly.

His bare fists sped up, punishing himself far more than the bag.

Come on, Scott. Drink me, drink me, drink me! the bottles in the garage's mini refrigerator seemed to sing.

Frustrated, he swung a right-hook with more power than he'd experienced in a decade. The flimsy chain snapped, sending the punching bag flying backward. He used his forearm to wipe the sweat from above his eyes.

"Screw you," he responded to his cravings. Sure, he'd gotten angry with Carol and, to a certain extent, Allison, but he also wanted to remain clearheaded. The power he derived from standing up to his addiction fueled him toward the house.

Gotta make this right, he thought as all the anger escaped his body.

He glanced toward the sinkhole – which was now covered by a tarp – and scowled. "It's all your fault," he whispered accusingly.

The tarp wrinkled with the blowing of the wind, and Scott could swear he'd heard whispering from deep in the ground. *Holy shit.* His pace quickened and his mind wandered back to childhood fears. Was there a monster living down there? And if so, what did it want?

"Carol," he called while stepping through the backdoor. "I'm sorry, babe. Can we talk?"

Carol braced herself. A quick scan of his voice didn't reveal the slur of too much alcohol, but she'd learned a long time ago that Scott's moods were unpredictable either way.

"We're in the living room," she replied.

The stench of Scott's physical exertions wafted into the room like an announcement. Carol and Allison unconsciously wrinkled their noses with disgust.

"What?" he barked before forcing himself to calm down again. "Sorry, I guess I do kind of stink. I'll shower in a minute, okay?"

Carol nodded, wondering what in the world he'd been up to.

As if reading her mind, he said, "I went a few rounds with the punching bag. Felt good. Damn good," he smiled.

"That's wonderful!" Carol said, only half faking her enthusiasm.

"What's that mean?" Allison asked.

"What's that mean? My god, I've failed as a parent," Scott said with as much joviality as he could summon. "It's the big brown bag hanging in the garage. It's for boxing."

"Boxing? Oh, you mean hitting people!" Allison lit up in a way that made Carol shift nervously.

Scott laughed and mussed up the top of his daughter's hair. "Yeah, I guess it is basically just hitting people. But what would *you* know about *that*, baby girl?"

"Nathan stole my ball a few weeks ago. I slugged him one in the gut!"

Carol's face contorted with shock and dismay. Scott, on the other hand, grinned at Allison.

"Then what happened?" he asked.

"He gave my ball back," Allison said proudly while literally wiping her hands clean at the memory.

"And you didn't get in trouble?" Carol asked.

"Nope!"

"Atta girl!" Scott said.

"What your father means," Carol said, "is that we're proud of you for standing up for yourself, but violence is wrong. You should never hit another person."

"But dad was boxing," Allison whined.

Finally picking up on Carol's attempt at being a good role model, Scott tried to back up his wife. "No, your mother is right. I was hitting a bag, not a person."

"But in boxing..." Allison tried before being interrupted.

"In boxing, both people have agreed to fight fairly by following rules."

"And if they break them?" she inquired.

"They get a penalty and maybe even lose."

"Even if they're the better fighter?"

"That's right, sweetheart."

"That's because doing the right thing is always more important than winning," Carol chimed in.

Scott forced himself not to roll his eyes.

Allison's face screwed up with the effort of considering this new information. "What if someone else breaks the rules first, though? Like by stealing?"

Damn, is she sharp, Scott thought proudly.

"Then you tell an adult and let them handle it," Carol said.

"Okay," Allison replied, followed by excusing herself from the room.

"What was it you wanted to say?" Carol asked her husband.

"I'm sorry about earlier."

"Okay."

"No, I mean it. I really am sorry. I don't know what the hell is going on, but I don't want to fight with you anymore."

She eyed him skeptically. "Have you been drinking?"

He bristled but held his tongue long enough to regain his composure. "No. Not a single drop."

"Keep it up, and then we'll talk."

He didn't appreciate what he took to be a dismissive tone, but Scott knew that saying anything else would be a losing battle. He issued a curt nod and headed to the shower.

CHAPTER ELEVEN

Princeton, WV

Ivy woke with a start. Somehow, despite her fear, she'd fallen asleep. Her face turned red as she realized her head was resting on Thad's shoulder, who was now awake.

I hope I didn't snore. Or, even worse, drool.

"Good morning," Thad said through a yawn.

"Morning?"

"Yeah, it's almost six-thirty," he responded.

"Oh my god," she sat up straight, causing her sleepy mind to feel a hint of whiplash. "I slept all night?"

"You needed it. And Rachel needed you to sleep, too. You can't help her if you're dead on your feet."

"Have the doctors..."

"She's out of surgery and doing well," he gently smiled. "They said she can't have any visitors until at least nine a.m., so I didn't see the point in waking you up."

She stretched and felt an irritating stiffness in her neck and shoulders. She wasn't entirely happy with his decision making on her behalf, but she could also see the wisdom in it.

"Thank you, Thad. Want some breakfast?"

"I thought you'd never ask. If I don't get some coffee in me soon, I'm going to turn into a monster," he chuckled.

They wandered into the almost empty hospital cafeteria with their stomachs complaining. Only one of the many restaurants was open.

"Starbucks it is, then," Ivy said.

A few moments later, they plopped down into uncomfortable chairs. But with coffee warming their hands and sugary sweets filling their mouths, they didn't pay much attention to the hospital's latest apparent attempt at keeping people from sitting still for too long.

"So, what's your story?" Ivy asked.

"Story? Um, nothing much. The usual, you know?"

"So, you live in Dunns, then?"

"I used to. My folks still have a small farm there, and I've been helping out for a few weeks."

"How'd you find us?"

Embarrassment colored his cheeks. "Honestly? My dad was fit to be tied when he saw you two." His voice dropped and aged as he imitated his father. "Look at those girls stomping across the land like they own it."

"Oh, no. Were we trespassing?"

"Not even a little bit," he said in his normal tone. "That's just my dad. He's always butting his nose in where it doesn't belong. Anyway, I went to check on you two to make sure you weren't lost. I'm glad I grabbed my rifle at the last second. There's lots of critters around there, and you never know when you might run into something nasty."

"I'm grateful. And I guess I should be thankful for your dad's suspiciousness, too."

"Yup, it saved the day for once. Not so sure we should tell him that, though. He'll just get even more intense with his 'stay off of my lawn' routine."

Now that she knew her sister was on the mend, Ivy allowed herself to notice their rescuer's good sense of humor. The rest of the package was appealing, too.

"You said you don't live around here anymore? Where are you from?"

"Ohio."

"Really?"

"Yeah," he looked at her, puzzled by her tone.

"That's crazy because we're from Ohio, too!"

"Whoa, that *is* crazy. What are the odds, right?"

What are the odds indeed? she pondered and began to look at him in a whole new light.

CHAPTER TWELVE

Centralia, PA

The news still played in Don's living room, but he'd abandoned it in favor of a different project. He now sat in a recliner facing the outside world. The living room window was open, with the screen removed. His shotgun sat on his lap, along with a pistol.

"We'll be ready," he whispered while stroking his shotgun.

Jill and Doreen's footsteps captured his attention. He brought the shotgun up to his shoulder and prepared to fire. Just before he could let loose, he recognized the two women.

"Ah, dammit," he muttered and lowered the gun. An evil light lit up his eyes as he reconsidered his options. The gun rose again, and he lined it up with Doreen.

Bang. Bang. Bang, he thought. *Maybe I should kill them. Damn sinners.*

The women walked out of view before he could decide. He soothed his wounded pride by reminding himself that there would be other chances.

♦ ♦ ♦

"I think I should go check on Don," Jill said.

"I don't know, hon," Doreen replied. "Doesn't the entire thing seem a bit, well, odd? I mean, him coming over here with a hurt foot, that awful smell...It doesn't seem safe."

"Oh, I really don't think he's going to do anything. You know his bark is worse than his bite. He was upset about his wife earlier. I feel bad leaving him alone."

"Let me come with you, then."

"It's not necessary, but if you insist..."

"I do," Doreen said decisively.

Jill rooted around in her medical bag for a few supplies. "Got it," she said to herself. "Okay, let's go."

The women walked back down the road they shared only with Don. As usual, their physical proximity widened as they got closer to his house. They no longer consciously thought about such acts; they simply happened out of habit.

Don spotted them and pumped his fist. "Oorah!" he chanted with pride. He'd been given a repeat of his first real test, and he wasn't going to fail. It was long past time to defend Centralia from everyone who would destroy it, and sinners were high on that list.

The shotgun sat against his shoulder once more. A bead of sweat dripped down his forehead. *Any second now.*

Doreen came into his sights first. *Good. Uppity bitch.* He took a deep breath, exhaled, and fired.

The roar of the shell kicking free of the shotgun shattered the street's normal solitude. Jill – who had attended to countless gunshot victims in her day – instantly pushed her wife to the ground before urging her to roll out of sight.

Did I get her? Don thought with bloodlust filling his mind.

Behind him, a color commentator urged viewers to take matters into their own hands. "This is biblical, people. Grab your guns and prepare to fight for what's rightfully yours. Stand your ground!"

"Yes!" Don shouted, so caught up in the moment that he tried to stand unassisted. "Shit!" His foot seemingly caught fire, sending vibrant pain signals to his brain that overrode everything else.

Taking advantage of the lull in shooting, Jill and Doreen positioned themselves where Don couldn't target them. Torn between fleeing and trying to deescalate the situation, Jill called out, "What *was* that, Don? An accident? It's okay if you had an accident."

"Shut up, bitch," he growled.

"I know you're hurting, Don, but this isn't the way to..."

"I said shut up!" he interrupted. "In case you didn't notice, the end of days has begun. And it's time to get rid of heathens like *you*."

"He's lost his damn mind," Doreen whispered. "We need to get out of here."

"Hang on a second," Jill said. "Don, what are you talking about?"

"I'm talking about God's wrath, you, you...lesbos!"

Despite the circumstances, Doreen and Jill had to cover their mouths to keep laughter from escaping. "Did he really just call us lesbos?" Doreen snickered. "Ooh, I'm *so* hurt."

Unaware of the sarcastic response, Don continued. "Flames shooting toward Heaven, the ground opening up and swallowing people whole. It's time for the righteous to take up arms."

"Did you read that in a tweet?" Doreen shouted derisively.

"I'm going to deliver you to Hell," he said before shooting indiscriminately out the window.

"Okay, we're out of here," Jill said and reached for Doreen's hand. They took off as quickly as their aging legs would carry them. Another blast from the shotgun made them jump, but they trusted that Don's injured foot would keep him from hitting his targets.

Thirty feet from home, a new roar filled the air. The ground shook as an unearthly cracking sound ripped apart the street in front of them. Steam hissed free of the expanding crack, and the women came to a halt.

"What the fuck?" Jill said under her breath.

The neighborhood continued to shake. A rush of air swooped down the road, followed by the shattering of glass. Doreen screamed and they fell to the ground.

"Oh, my lord," Doreen said. She began crab-walking backward and yelled for Jill to do the same.

The split in the earth extended past the concrete, eating up the empty lots of grass to both sides of them. Flames leaped free of the newly formed fissure, leaving the women with no choice but to move closer to Don's house.

Sensing them near, he fired again.

"Don, we don't have time for this foolishness, dammit!" Jill projected her voice as loud as she could, in the hopes of being heard over the increasing din. "The entire road is collapsing. We have to get out of here, now. All of us."

He stopped shooting and truly took in his environment. *When did everything start shaking?* Most of his personal belongings laid scattered on the floor as if they'd been knocked over by a powerful earthquake.

I don't need them. He hopped toward the front door, determined to get in his truck and drive off without his neighbors. A bookcase wobbled unseen to his right as he gathered his guns and keys.

A new rumble swept through the ground, moving everything unsecured like a big ocean wave pounding against sand castles. Don fell and soon found himself under the weight of his heavy oak bookcase. He tried in vain to push it off.

"Please help me," he begged his creator. "I'm your tool! Don't leave me like this." Tears filled his eyes and panic stoked the flames of his hatred. *This is their fault.*

"Don? Are you okay?" Jill's voice barely reached his ears.

"Why are we doing this?" Doreen asked.

"He has the only vehicle, remember?"

Jill twisted the front door knob and found it unlocked. "Don, I'm going to come in and get you. Please don't shoot. We want to help you get out of here."

She pushed the door inward and saw his prone frame. Her nursing instincts kicked in and she rushed to his side.

"Doreen, help me lift this."

The women struggled with the bookcase, but eventually flipped it off of Don. He grimaced as one of the shelves cracked. *Damn them.*

"We're going to get you out of here," Jill said.

They each reached for a side and attempted to haul him up.

"Don't touch me!" he shrieked.

"Don," Doreen said impatiently, "we're not going to give you the gay or whatever it is you're worried about, goddammit. Now get up, you stubborn, foolish man, before we leave you to die."

The kiss of flames grew ever closer to Don's property line, and he reasoned that leaving with them now was his best choice. He could always dispose of them later, after all. He begrudgingly allowed himself to be helped to the truck. They left the shotgun sitting on the living room floor, but neither woman noticed that he stuck a pistol into the back of his waistband.

"Holy Hell," Don uttered as cinders scorched his clothes.

Half the block had disappeared. In its place stood the widest, longest, deepest road fissure he'd ever seen. It made Graffiti Highway look like a joke. The flames shooting free of the gaping maw also dwarfed those he'd witnessed earlier.

Before anyone had a chance to put on their seatbelt – or even shut their car door all the way – Jill's foot pressed the truck's pedal down to the floor. The truck bucked, then shot forward. New cracks appeared in the asphalt, strained by the vehicle's weight.

All the blood drained out of Jill's knuckles. She swerved left and right like an agitated bumblebee, trying desperately to avoid falling into any of the newly formed pits of fire.

CHAPTER THIRTEEN

Southgate, MI

"Scott?" Carol called.

"Yeah?" he said as he wrapped a towel around his waist.

"Would you come out here, please?"

"On my way." He heard the strain in her voice and knew she had something important to share with him. He also understood that she didn't want Allison to know about whatever was on her mind.

"What's up?" Scott asked.

Her already light skin had turned bone white. She pointed toward the television.

"...initial reports indicate that the ghost town has become completely engulfed in flames. The images you see on your screen come courtesy of Twitter user..."

"What in the world?" He sunk to his knees in front of the TV, enraptured by photos that conjured up memories of Southern

California's biggest and deadliest wildfires. He opened his mouth to ask a question, but shut it as the ticker at the bottom of the screen told him everything he needed to know.

"Centralia? Why do I know that name?" he asked.

"It's that town with the mine fire. The one that inspired *Silent Hill*," Carol responded shakily.

"But I thought…"

"Yeah, me too. They have no idea how the fire got so big again. It's worse than ever, according to the news."

"You're not kidding," he said. "It looks like something out of a movie."

"An apocalyptic movie," she whispered. "Is this really the end of days?"

Gathering his courage, he sat next to her on the couch and wrapped his arm around her shoulders. After kissing her forehead, he tried to placate her nerves.

"I'm sure it's just some type of natural disaster or something. I mean, they always said it would take decades for the coal to burn out, right? Something must have sped up the process. Hell, maybe it was even fracking," he said, happy to return to one of his normal arguments. "Or some idiots poured gasoline into the ground or something."

Her eyes sought out the truth behind his words. Could it possibly be true? She cringed at the lack of conviction in his gaze. They both knew something bigger was happening. And whatever it was, it seemed to be spreading awfully quickly.

Afraid to provoke his anger, she hesitated before returning to an earlier question. "Should we leave?"

"I don't know," he sighed. "Your car is fueled up...but go where? Seems like stuff is starting to happen everywhere, doesn't it?"

She didn't remind him that Michigan and one town in Pennsylvania were the sole places hit so far – at least to their knowledge – nor did she mention that both states had suffered from different events. In her gut, she knew his words were accurate. This wasn't something they could just outrun. And who knew how much worse things might be in another town or state?

"We should probably gather some supplies just in case, though," Scott said.

"Like what?"

"What do those prepper dudes always say? Something about a bug out bag..." he said to himself. "Oh, yeah. Water, food, first-aid kit, stuff like that."

"A bug out bag?" Despite her fear, she couldn't stop her long-held disdain for preppers from altering her tone.

His eyes turned sharp for half a beat before softening. "I know, I know. You think those guys are nuts. But they may have a point. If nothing else, they certainly know how to pack for a camping trip, right?"

She chuckled and found herself warming to the idea. "Okay, let's grab a few things. But try to keep it from Allison, at least for now. I don't want her to worry."

"Roger that," he said.

She opened the cupboard and noticed for the first time how much of their food required a stove. Frustrated, she tossed some granola bars, a loaf of bread, and some cereal into an old duffel bag. None of this would get them far. She hoped that Scott still remembered how to hunt, while simultaneously trying to convince herself it would never come to that.

"Hey Scott?"

"Yeah?"

"Make sure you pack your hunting gear."

Surprise jolted his frame. She'd always hated it that he hunted, so he'd stopped a few years ago. Her insistence had driven yet another wedge between them, but he'd still decided it was easier to give up on the hobby than to have yet another thing to fight about.

He hated to admit it, but he'd always known she was smarter and more rational than him. If she wanted him to gather his hunting gear now, she must be even more concerned than she was letting on. That thought terrified him almost as much as the sinkhole in their backyard.

CHAPTER FOURTEEN

Princeton, WV

"How do you feel?" Ivy asked.

"Like a truck ran over me, backed up, and ran over me again," Rachel said with a whisper of weakened breath.

"The doctor said you'll recover," Ivy smiled while gently stroking her twin's hair.

"Do me a favor," Rachel said.

"Anything."

"Don't *ever* talk about genealogy again."

The sisters shared a laugh. Ivy's spirits rose. If Rachel could already make jokes, she was definitely on the mend. Between that and whatever was brewing between herself and Thad, Ivy had a good reason to look on the bright side.

"So, what the hell was that deer doing, anyway?" Rachel asked.

"They're not really sure. They ran some tests on you, and they all came back negative. But you're still going to need a full course of rabies treatments, I'm afraid."

"Ugh," Rachel said. "That's just perfect."

"Sorry, sis."

"You'd better be," Rachel teased. "How's it going on your end? Bored to death yet?"

"Actually, no. Thad stayed, and he's been great company."

"Thad?"

"He's the guy who saved you."

"I don't even remember that," Rachel said. "Is he cute?"

Ivy's cheeks grew hot.

"Oh damn, he *is,* isn't he?"

"Yeah," Ivy admitted.

"Then what are you doing sitting here talking to me? I'm really tired anyway, so get out of here. You're banished. Don't come back until you have something juicy to share with me."

"Are you sure?" Ivy asked.

Rachel yawned in confirmation.

"I'll check on you again soon," Ivy kissed her sister's forehead. Rachel began snoring lightly by the time Ivy reached the door.

She wandered back down the hallways, turning left, then right. Butterflies pushed free of the cocoons inside her stomach when she spotted Thad. Could there truly be something between them?

He waved in greeting as she approached. The pounding of footsteps caught her off guard, and she spun toward the hospital entrance.

"Clear out, clear out!" a burly EMT shouted. A man covered in blood writhed in agony on a gurney.

Ivy tried to move, but her feet froze to the spot when a second gurney followed close behind the first. Thad raced to her side and helped pull her out of each gurney's path.

"It fucking bit me!" one of the patients yelled before disappearing into the emergency room.

CHAPTER FIFTEEN

Ashland, PA

"Stop the truck, dammit!" Don yelled for the third time.

It had been close, but the unlikely trio had managed to leave Centralia behind without sustaining any serious damage to Don's vehicle. But with the flames – and the ghost town – a mere three miles behind them, Jill didn't want to stop yet. Especially not in the ominously named Ashland, which experts had long predicted would eventually succumb to the coal fire raging underground.

"Hush!" Doreen snapped back. "We just saved your life, you miserable old coot."

"Who asked you to?" he flared. "I'd rather die than be saved by the likes of you."

"That can be arranged," Jill said with a terseness Doreen had never heard before. Testing his bluff, Jill made a U-turn and started flooring it back toward Centralia.

"What are you doing?" Doreen asked quietly.

"Exactly what he asked for," Jill answered.

Don's incredulous expression grew slack as the flames came back into view.

"Should I drop you off here, or would you like me to take you back to your house?" Derision dripped from each of Jill's words.

"You're a crazy bitch," he said in a subdued tone. "Now turn us back around."

"Oh, you mean you *do* want us to save you? Because I thought you didn't. You're sending me mixed signals here, Don."

His fingers inched toward the pistol resting against his lower back.

"Knock it off," he growled.

"Whatever," Jill said as she turned the truck back toward Ashland.

"Where are we going to go?" Doreen asked.

"As far as we can get," her wife said.

The pickup truck sped down Centre Street. Doreen gazed longingly at a convenience store. She was thirsty, hungry, and needed a bathroom. The memory of the flames – combined with the pungent smoke that had already made its way into Ashland – made it clear that this wasn't a good time for a pitstop, though.

They made it to the edge of the borough before an Ashland police cruiser signaled for them to pull over. For the first time in her life, Jill ignored the law. The speedometer crept even higher as she attempted to lose the officer.

"Are you kidding me?" Officer Rand said to himself. "Not on my watch."

The overzealous officer's speed picked up. He barked into his radio about the need for backup, knowing that only one other officer was on duty. Luck was with the department that day, and the two police cars were soon positioned behind and in front of the speeding truck.

"Dammit!" Jill exclaimed as she pulled the truck to a stop. "We don't have time for this."

Officer Rand stepped up to the driver's side window and said, "What's the rush, ma'am?"

"Centralia is on fire!" she blurted out. "And it's headed here next."

He cocked his head to the side, ostensibly considering her words, but actually taking a closer look inside the truck.

"She's not kidding, officer," Doreen piped up. "Look!" She pointed toward a black plume of smoke that grew closer by the moment.

"What's going on here?" Officer Rand asked Don.

Don smirked at the cop's deference toward a fellow male.

"Well...Centralia *is* burning, that much is true. Aside from that, though? I asked these crazy chicks half-a-dozen times to stop. This is my truck, by the way. Mine," he pointed toward his chest. "They seem to think they can do whatever they want just because I've got a messed-up foot. I didn't ask for this. They forced it on me."

"I'm going to need you to follow me," Officer Rand commanded.

"But officer..." Jill began.

"Shut it! I'm not going to tell you again. You either follow me, or I'll toss your asses into the backseat of my cruiser. Got it?"

"Yes, officer," she said sullenly.

During the short drive to the police station, Doreen said, "I hope you know it's your fault if we all die now, Don."

He chortled. "I'm not going die, bitch. I was the victim here. They'll take my statement and let me go. You two, though? By the time I'm done, they'll lock you up for taking me hostage and stealing my truck. Looks like today is judgment day, ladies. Are you ready to meet your maker?"

CHAPTER SIXTEEN

Southgate, MI

"Should we wake her up?" Carol whispered.

"No, let her sleep," Scott said. "I'll go get her."

He sneaked into his daughter's room and carefully picked her up. Things had gotten much worse in Metro Detroit during the past few hours, and he and Carol had decided it was now or never.

Allison stirred slightly before clutching her red stuffed BunnieKittie closer to her chest. The plush animal toy had always seemed a bit odd to Scott with its black X's for eyes and Frankenstein's monster-type stitches. But Allison had fallen in love with it immediately a couple of years ago, and she refused to sleep without it.

"Oh, good!" Carol said quietly at the sight of BunnieKittie. This trip was already going to be difficult enough, and she didn't even want to imagine the ruckus that would have been caused by forgetting Allison's favorite toy.

With their daughter sleeping in the backseat, Scott maneuvered the vehicle down their small suburban street. They didn't live in the town's best neighborhood, but it was also far from the worst. Or at least it had been until all hell started breaking loose.

Within the past six hours, several more sinkholes had appeared in their general area. People were getting scared, as evidenced by fires and signs of looting. Scott had to swerve around a virtual minefield of potholes and small sinkholes that threatened to completely destroy the asphalt.

Scott paused at the end of the block to check for traffic. The car vibrated under the pressure of a neighbor's golf club beating against the trunk.

"What the?" Scott said.

"Drive. Drive!"

Their tires squealed as they turned right and were met almost immediately by a sinkhole.

"Jesus," Scott mumbled.

Carol shot him a look but kept her criticism to herself. Besides, she was just glad he was behind the wheel. She risked a glance into the backseat and smiled at her daughter's sleeping frame. *That kid could sleep through anything.*

"That clinches it," Scott said as flames and smoke swirled around them on both sides of Eureka Road. "We need to get as far away from people as possible. The U.P. it is."

Carol didn't disagree with his assessment, but anxiety shot through her system at the thought of making it all the way to

Michigan's Upper Peninsula. On the best of days, it took four to five hours to get there, plus several hours more to truly leave most of civilization behind. If sinkholes filled their route, who knew how long it would take?

CHAPTER SEVENTEEN

Princeton, WV

Chaos had quickly overwhelmed the hospital. More than a dozen new bite victims had been checked in during a single shift, and no one was quite sure how to help them. Rachel's recovery had been the smoothest so far. Rumors swirled around the waiting room that at least one of the new patients had already died.

Ivy paced up and down the halls with Thad at her side.

"We can't leave her here," she said.

"Doesn't she need another rabies shot soon?"

"Yeah, but I've got a very bad feeling about all of this. It's like something is telling me – no, yelling at me – that we need to get out of here ASAP."

A nurse shuffled past them. His bloodshot eyes caught their attention.

"Did that seem...?"

"Much worse than tired eyes? Yes," Thad said. "Okay, I'm on board. What do we do?"

Screams echoed down the hall from the latest round of bite victims. Another nurse rushed past them, muttering something about being almost out of beds.

"There's not enough staff here to deal with all of this," Ivy said. "Discharging Rachel will probably make them happy."

Determined to try this route, she marched down to Rachel's room. Her sister was polishing off a green Jell-O cup.

"Hey!" Rachel said. "And you must be Thad," she practically purred.

"Wow, you look better," Ivy remarked. "Feel like getting out of here?"

"Do I ever!"

Ivy and Thad disconnected the IV and all the sensors. Rachel got back into her clothes and they were headed toward the door when a nurse walked in.

"Oh! You shouldn't be out of bed, miss."

"Why not? I feel great!" Rachel said.

Puzzled, the nurse responded, "Please, sit back down. Let me check your vitals."

Confusion clouded the nurse's face as every test came back with normal numbers. "Isn't that the damndest thing you ever saw?"

"Please, we need to get her out of here," Ivy cut in. "The hospital is swarming with patients, and some of them look *really* bad."

"Your sister needs another rabies shot tomorrow. Let her rest for another day, then we'll get a doctor to examine her again. They'll probably release her then."

The patient in the bed next to Rachel's coughed, then sputtered. "Help," she managed to wheeze out before falling to the floor.

"Oh, my!" the nurse said as she pulled the dividing curtain aside. The woman had passed out in a small pool of her own blood. Her lips were red-speckled from coughing, and her limbs twitched.

"We're getting out of here. Now," Ivy said forcefully.

The nurse stood torn between both patients. She pressed a button for assistance. "Wait one minute. I won't stop you. I swear." She disappeared and reappeared so fast that the group hadn't had time to ignore her request.

"Here." The nurse thrust a small bag of medical supplies into Ivy's hands. "Get out while you still can. There's a rabies shot in there. Administer it according to the directions tomorrow. She'll need to get to another medical facility four days later for the third shot."

"Thank you," Ivy said.

Ivy, Thad, and Rachel pushed their way out of the room mere seconds before a team of nurses raced inside to help the other patient.

"Should we check out at the front desk?" Rachel asked.

"I don't think so," Ivy responded after spotting the long line of people clamoring for an intake form.

They dodged small spatters of coughed up blood while walking to the exit. Outside, the situation turned more dire; every parking spot was occupied, and at least a dozen more vehicles were looking for a place to park.

CHAPTER EIGHTEEN

Ashland, PA

Officer Rand scowled at Jill and Doreen. They'd just told their story for the third time, including Jill's explanation for why she hadn't stopped when he'd first tried to pull her over.

"Something isn't adding up here. You were driving someone else's truck – who says you basically took him hostage – and you refused to stop, even though there weren't flames at your heels. What made you think speeding away from a police officer was a wise choice?"

Jill closed her eyes and counted to three. "It's like I said, officer, the fire destroyed our block within minutes, and it showed no signs of stopping. With the coal under Ashland, we figure it's only a matter of time before it catches up to us. I admit I made a mistake when I didn't pull over right away, but I was terrified.

"And Don's not playing straight with you. I bet he didn't tell you that he fired several shots at us for no good reason before our street broke open. Or that we still pulled a wooden bookcase off of him and helped him get away from the fire.”

The officer’s eyes turned hard. “Now see, that’s what I’m talking about. None of that makes any sense. Normal people don’t go to the aid of those who’re shooting at them. Why would you do that?”

“I’m a retired nurse, officer. It’s in my blood to help people, no matter what.”

“And?” Officer Rand prompted her.

“And, yes, he also has the only working vehicle in town. But he’s got a fractured foot, too, so he wasn’t exactly going to be getting anywhere fast without our help.”

“Did he say you could take his truck?”

“Well, not in those words, no. But he came with us of his own accord.”

“He wants to press charges against you.”

“For what?” she said incredulously.

“Grand theft auto.”

“That’s ridiculous!”

“Perhaps...but I can’t shake the feeling that there’s a lot you’re not telling me. And you’ve admitted to taking the vehicle without getting the owner’s permission. I’m afraid my hands are tied, for the moment.” The officer’s conciliatory commentary didn’t reach his eyes, which took on a predatory stare. “I’ve got no choice but to lock the two of you up.”

“No! You can’t do that. You’re going to get us killed!”

"Settle down, ma'am," he said tersely. "And put your arms behind your back."

She leaped free of her chair and ran toward the lobby. She made it five paces before the city's other officer slammed her against a desk. Stunned and temporarily unable to breathe, she couldn't defend herself as he slapped a cold pair of handcuffs far too tightly around her wrists.

"Jill!" Doreen called out in horror.

Officer Rand entered the lobby and motioned toward Doreen. "Unless you want the same treatment, I suggest you walk your ass over here right now and surrender. You're both under arrest."

Defeated, Doreen slumped over to Officer Rand. He cuffed her and firmly grabbed onto her arm. She craned her neck backward long enough to see the cruel laughter contorting Don's face.

The women were marched to the city's sole holding cell, uncuffed, and shoved inside. Their hopes of survival shattered as the heavy, metal barred door slammed shut.

CHAPTER NINETEEN

Flint, MI

Traffic conditions on I-75 N hadn't been as bad as expected after they passed through Detroit. But it had still taken them almost three hours to reach Flint instead of the typical seventy-five minutes.

They had no intention of stopping now, especially after spotting a disturbing array of fires just off the freeway. The number of sinkholes on I-75 also increased, leaving Scott swerving the wheel from one side to the other like a drunken teenager.

The only good thing about the trip so far was Allison's steady snoring from the backseat. Carol knew it wouldn't last forever, but the longer she could hold off on having to explain all of this to her daughter, the better.

She switched the radio back on and scanned for a local AM news channel. Static ruled most of the airwaves until the middle of the dial.

"...stay in your homes. Do not, I repeat, do not go outside. Please reserve all calls to 911 and your local police station for serious emergencies. The governor has also requested that people reduce their usage of phones at this time to help ease the burden on the circuits and towers..."

"Do you think we made a mistake?" Carol asked her husband.

"No," he grunted while yanking the wheel to the right. "They're just saying that stuff to prevent a panic. Everyone who listens is a sitting duck."

She quietly pondered his words for a few moments. Carol wanted nothing more than to be back in their small track home nestled in the middle of their lower middle-class neighborhood. Yet at the same time, she knew staying hadn't been an option.

Hell, the house she kept pining for might not even be standing anymore. She'd already seen several wrecked homes during their drive and understood that nowhere was truly safe. The comforts of home were now relegated to the land of the idyllic American dream; long since extinct, at least for people like Carol and her family.

Smoke from the fires lingered long after Scott's skillful driving took them far past the source of the flames. They found themselves traveling through an area of Michigan that wasn't as populated, and this seemed to appease whatever had been causing all the sinkholes. With a smoother road ahead of them, Scott pushed the pedal down and hurled his family into the night.

CHAPTER TWENTY

Dunns, WV

Thad agreed with Ivy and Rachel that getting far away from Princeton – and Dunns – was a high priority. However, his concern for his parents forced the trio to make a pit stop in the town where their crazy misadventure had begun.

"Sorry about this," he said for at least the fifth time. "I wish my parents weren't so opposed to cell phones."

The truck came to a halt on a dirt driveway facing a well-maintained farm house.

"I'll just be a couple of minutes," Thad said as he hopped out. The gravel crunched under his feet. He tried to silence the voice of doom that currently played on a loop inside his mind.

"Mom? Dad?" His voice rang through the house but was met by an eerie hush. Panicked, he darted through every room, then rushed out the back door toward the barn.

Darkness permeated the barn's interior until his fumbling hand found a light switch. A pool of red liquid on the far side of the barn quickened his pace and his pulse. *Please no,* he mentally begged the world.

The shallow pool looked and smelled like blood, but there didn't appear to be any source for it. Puzzled, he glanced around until something dripped on his head. Frustrated by the old structure's constant leaks, he absentmindedly wiped the moisture from his head. His hand dropped in front of his face on its way back to his side, and he barely suppressed the shriek that threatened to rip free of his throat.

Looking up at the loft, he saw a trickle of blood dripping over the side and through the slats. Terrified of knowing – and equally afraid of merely walking away – he adroitly climbed the ladder before his nerve could completely abandon him.

His mom's chewed up face stared past him with sightless eyes. Lying next to her was the lifeless form of his dad, who had died with a pitchfork buried deep in his stomach. Sickened, he turned around and unleashed a torrent of vomit before more closely examining his mom's wounds.

Although he couldn't say for sure, some of the bites looked porcine in nature. *If that's the case...*he flew down the ladder and threw himself across the yard. The distinctive grunting and snorting of pigs soon rose from behind Thad's heels.

Even on their worst days, these animals were far swifter than most people would believe, especially at sprinting. If he hesitated or stumbled even slightly, he'd never get back up. With this certainty burning in his mind, he pushed himself even harder.

Ivy spotted his difficulty and slid into the driver's seat. The truck rumbled to life, and she quickly spun around and backed up in Thad's direction. Immediately grasping her plan, Thad put on one more burst of energy as the truck stopped a few feet away. He jumped for the tailgate and pulled himself into the truck bed, relieved that he'd removed the cover a few days ago.

He banged his hand down three times against the truck to signal Ivy to take off. Tires ripped up the grass and sent mud flying. The lead pigs reached the vehicle as it began to move. Enraged at losing their prey, they threw themselves against the back bumper.

Goosebumps dotted Thad's flesh as he envisioned his pursuers somehow climbing into the truck bed after them. Maybe they'd even climb on top of each other's backs until one of them was high enough to leap on board. His awful daydream failed to come true due to Ivy's quick thinking behind the wheel.

CHAPTER TWENTY-ONE

Ashland, PA

Officer Rand had almost completed his interview with Don when the phone rang.

"Ashland PD. This is Officer Rand."

Confusion crossed his face. "Slow down, Ben. What's happening, again?" Rand listened intently and battled to keep his voice and expressions neutral.

"I'm on it. Thanks for calling. And Ben? Be safe."

He dropped the phone's receiver into the cradle and yelled for his partner. Don started to stand up in response to the activity, but Rand motioned for him to sit back down.

"I need you to wait here, sir. We'll be back in a few minutes." Rand walked toward the exit before turning back around. He quietly picked up Don's keys from his desk and pocketed them before leaving.

Gotta make sure he doesn't bolt on me.

Don waited until the police cruiser left before hobbling his way back to the holding cell.

"Looks like you ladies are shit out of luck," he laughed with a humorless stare. "Something big is going on in town, and I bet you'll only need one guess to figure it out. That fire's coming for you."

"That means it's coming for you, too," Jill shot back.

"Maybe, but I'm out here, and you're stuck in there. The cops took off, which means you're not going anywhere."

"They can't just leave us like this," Doreen said. Her voice rose in tandem with her growing sense of terror.

"Seems like they can do whatever they want, and they've already done it," Don replied with a smirk. "Well, ladies, I guess I'd better be on my way."

"Dammit, Don! Leaving us to die isn't going to please God," Jill bartered.

"Hah! That shows how much you know. God doesn't protect the likes of you. Enjoy your barbeque."

Jill and Doreen continued to shout after Don, but he no longer cared to hear their pleading and threatening commentary. After a few painful moments of maneuvering back through the small station, he stood in front of Rand's desk.

"Now, where did he put my keys?" Don muttered. He'd seen the officer toss his keys on the desk, but now they didn't appear to be anywhere in sight. He shifted through Rand's papers a few times before conceding that they weren't there.

Cursing under his breath, Don hopped behind the desk and opened the top drawer. No keys. Flustered, he opened every other drawer that wasn't locked.

"Where are they?" he whined, finally realizing he might be in some serious trouble.

Ten minutes later, Don slumped back onto the bench in the lobby. His keys had either disappeared or Rand had taken them with him.

What kind of garbage would do something like that? Leave me here without my keys when I didn't do anything wrong? I'll have his badge for this! Or maybe...could this be another test from God?

He looked upward and said, "I understand, my Lord. Rand is just another nasty sinner. I'll take care of him for you when he returns."

CHAPTER TWENTY-TWO

Pinconning, MI

Scott exited the freeway. If it had been up to him, he would have driven straight through to the U.P., but the car needed gas and his wife desperately needed a bathroom. Maneuvering around a tiny sinkhole, he pulled up to the only accessible pump.

Although the lot contained only one other car – presumably owned by an employee – the lights were on and everything seemed to work properly. Carol hesitated about whether or not to wake up Allison. *Who knows when we'll be able to stop like this again? I'd better wake her.*

Allison stirred, stretching and moaning before opening her eyes.

"Mom? Where are we? Why am I in the car?"

"I'll explain everything in a few minutes, sweetie. Do you need to go to the bathroom?"

Allison wearily nodded and stumbled out of the car. Carol grabbed her hand and they shuffled inside the empty station.

"Hello?" Carol called out. "We're getting gas and need to use the restroom."

They waited for a few seconds before the call of nature urged Carol forward. The lady's room wouldn't open. *Maybe that's where the cashier is?* Unwilling to wait any longer, Carol knocked on the men's room, then slowly opened the door.

"Come with me."

"But it's a one-seater, Mom."

"I know...I just, well, I'd feel a lot better if you stayed with me."

Confused, Allison acquiesced.

By the time they exited a few minutes later, Scott was waiting for his turn. "Have you seen anyone, babe?"

"No, but the lady's room is locked. Maybe the cashier got sick or something."

"You two go ahead and head out. I'll be there in a minute." He handed her the keys.

"You heard your dad. Let's go," she said before pausing. "Hey, wait a minute. Don't you think we should pick up some supplies while we're here?"

"From who?" Scott's voice rang out from behind the bathroom door.

Ignoring this comment, Carol grabbed some water from the cooler and picked up a few bags of chips and peanuts. She placed them on the counter and spotted a bell to ring for service.

Ah! They must be in the back somewhere.

The chime of the bell failed to produce any results. Queasy about the idea of stealing, she pulled a ten-dollar bill out of her pocket and sat it on the counter. To even out the exchange, she encouraged Allison to pick out a few more items. With Scott's help, they carried their haul to the car and drove away.

The newly silent gas station hummed with electricity. If Carol or Scott had still been there, they might have noticed an odd dripping sound coming from the lady's room. They surely would have spotted the red trail of liquid that started to seep under the door within fifteen minutes of their departure.

The gas station attendant's bite wound hadn't healed as she'd expected. Instead, the dog bite had bled through Lila's gauze bandages. Somewhere between noticing this and going to the restroom to clean up, Lila's life had changed forever. Now she'd never get the chance to travel to Europe as she'd always dreamed...or to do anything else, for that matter.

CHAPTER TWENTY-THREE

Dunns, WV

"Are you all right, Thad?" Ivy asked.

His pulse hadn't stopped racing yet, despite being two miles down the road and finally back inside the safety of the truck's cab.

"I...I guess so," he replied without any conviction.

"What *was* that?" Rachel said.

"The pigs have gone mad. Th-they killed my parents." Anguish twisted his face and he made no effort to stop his eyes from overflowing with tears.

Ivy reached over and took his hand. "I'm so sorry."

Thad leaned toward Ivy, and she wrapped her arms around him. Her hand stroked the nape of his neck as his sobs soaked her shirt. *What the hell is happening?* she wondered.

"We should get going," Rachel chimed in tremulously. Sweat dripped from her pale forehead, and she found it impossible to keep her mouth moist. Unwilling to express these issues to the others, she remained silent until long after they'd merged onto I-77 N.

Twenty miles had passed in the truck's rearview mirror before Ivy brought the vehicle to a halt again. Traffic snarled the freeway, making it clear the word had gotten out: Something strange was happening, and everyone who'd gotten a glimpse of it wanted to flee for their lives.

"Rachel?" Ivy asked.

'Yeah, sis?"

"Can you get online?"

Rachel's eyes narrowed dubiously while taking in the single bar on her screen. The loading icon spun so long it made her dizzy, compounding the queasy sensation in her stomach and chest. She clicked the phone off as a single image loaded.

"Oh!" She quickly turned the screen back on. Her brows furrowed as she struggled to make sense of the viral video screenshot on her homepage.

"Um, guys?" Rachel began. "This is much bigger than we thought."

"What's going on?" Ivy asked.

Thad sucked in his breath unconsciously, certain that the sky was about to fall on their heads.

"There are sinkholes all over Michigan," Rachel announced.

"Shit," Thad whispered.

"Anything else?" Ivy said.

"I'm waiting for it to load...wait, here's something. Oh my god. I guess part of Pennsylvania is on fire? Looks like all the local hospitals are overrun, too."

Rachel's pale face flushed and a new round of sweat dotted her forehead.

"Are you okay?" Thad asked.

"Yeah, I'm fine," Rachel said with a hint of evasiveness. "It's ridiculous how hot it is, though. Turn the A/C on, sis."

Ivy and Thad reached for the air conditioner knob at the same time. A pleasant tingling announced the midair collision of their hands. Distracted, neither noticed that Rachel's breathing had become a bit shallow, accompanied by a lack of focus in her eyes.

"Looks like we're going to be stuck here for a while," Ivy said.

"I think I'll take a nap," Rachel said as her energy continued to wane.

"Sounds good. You need to get more rest, anyway. We'll wake you up if anything happens."

Rachel's exhausted frame issued a slight snore before Ivy finished speaking.

CHAPTER TWENTY-FOUR

Ashland, PA

Smoke flitted into the police station through the closed entry door. Don wrung his hands, alternating between terror and anger. He'd torn the station apart, but his keys remained elusive.

What now?

Doreen coughed from the holding cell and his face lit up.

It sure will be good to see those uppity bitches get what's coming to them.

"Don? Let's make a deal, okay? You let us out, and we'll help you get to safety again. No hard feelings," Jill's voice trembled.

He hesitated. On the one hand, he wanted to be strong enough to serve God's will. But at the same time, he didn't see how he could continue to act as God's agent if he died, too.

"How do you plan to do that?" Don asked. "My keys aren't here, and I doubt you're going to carry me out of town."

"I can get your truck started," Doreen said while wheezing.

"What's that?" Don asked.

"Do you remember that hunk of junk we used to have?"

"You mean the foreign piece of shit you two drove before you got your latest betrayal to American workers? Yeah, I remember."

Ignoring his commentary, Doreen said, "By the end, the ignition didn't work right. That'll teach you to hotwire a car really quick. If we can find a screwdriver, it'll be even easier."

"I knew you two were always up to no good," he scowled. Still, this could be his only chance to save his own skin. Should he take it?

Don paused long enough to have a mental conversation with God. With a nod, he thanked the almighty for confirming what he already knew; he must stay alive long enough to clear the area of sinners.

The smoke thickened and Doreen launched into another coughing fit.

"All right, all right. Hold your horses," Don said. "I think I saw the cell key around here somewhere."

He worked his way back through the mess he'd made of Rand's desk. "Ah ha! Here it is." He crossed the station and stood before the cell, holding Jill and Doreen's temporary salvation in his hand.

"You see this, ladies? It means you listen to me this time, got it?"

Barely containing the urge to roll her eyes, Jill agreed to Don's terms. His demented, rictus grin almost made her regret her decision, but anything had to be better than burning to death, right?

The cell lock popped open, and both women pushed the steel bars open in their rush to escape.

"Did you spot a screwdriver anywhere, Don?" Doreen asked.

"Huh? Oh, yeah. There's one in the top desk drawer," he pointed, without making any move to help.

Frustrated, Doreen raced to the desk and unceremoniously dumped the entire top drawer's contents on the ground. The screwdriver gleamed from within the pile. She grabbed it, plus a pair of pliers for good measure.

"Aren't you forgetting something?" Don yelled gruffly as Doreen tried to exit the station. "The two of you have to take me with you. Trust me when I say that you don't want to find out what'll happen if you don't."

"I was just trying to…"

"Shut it, and get over here," he interrupted. His hands itched to remove the gun from his back waistband.

The women shared a disdainful glance but returned to Don's side. Gripping both their shoulders, he found it easier to hop through the door and over to his truck.

Flames had obliterated the road less than two blocks away and were on their way to the police station. Jill and Doreen struggled beneath Don's weight and the scorching blast of the approaching fire. With several grunts and a few choice words, they managed to ferry their burden to his truck.

Doreen breathed a sigh of relief as the door handle opened without any protests. *Thank goodness he didn't lock the door.* She hadn't told anyone else, but Doreen's abilities did not extend to breaking into cars.

Using her tools, Doreen went to work. Instead of opening the wire panel like Don expected, she jammed the screwdriver into the ignition.

"Hey, what are you doing?"

Ignoring him, Doreen spun the handle of the screwdriver in a full circle several times with as much speed as she could muster. Finally, a cracking sound greeted her from inside the ignition column. Pleased to have successfully imitated a process that usually required a drill, she removed the screwdriver before sticking it back in much more carefully. With a quick turn of the tool, the truck came to life.

Jill whooped with appreciation. Don blustered through a long list of derogatory comments and rude questions. Doreen didn't pay much attention to either of them as she put the vehicle in gear and haphazardly left the station's parking lot.

The fire had gained a lot of ground since the trio last checked on it. Flames stood a mere half-block away as they made their second close escape.

They passed through Locustdale and Locust Gap without slowing down. *Appropriate,* Doreen mused about each town's name. *Between the fire and Don, it sure feels like a plague.* She made a left to stay on PA-901, hoping that putting a few twists and turns between them and the fire would remove them from harm's way.

Doreen slammed on the brakes just past the 'Welcome to Excelsior' sign. More than eight miles separated them from Ashland, and she couldn't stand the thought of delaying her plan any longer.

"Help me, Jill," she said.

Confused, Jill followed Doreen out of the truck. They conferred quietly for a moment before reaching for Don.

"Don't touch me," he shrieked as the women began lifting his heavy bulk. "This is my truck, dammit. You can't dump me and steal it. I won't let you!"

Despite everything, Jill's heart sat heavily in her chest. It didn't feel right to leave someone like this, but she knew Doreen had a point when she'd said, "We have to take care of ourselves first. You know he's going to stab us in the back the first chance he gets. Probably literally."

Before they could get him outside, Don startled them with his gun. "Put me back this instant or I'll shoot you both between the eyes."

They did as he commanded, then turned to walk away. A shot ripped past Jill's shoulder.

"You ladies are even dumber than I thought. Get your asses back in this truck and drive. Don't make me say it again. Remember, I don't need both of you to get me out of here. And I don't need either of you after that."

The threat put speed into their retreat. Seconds later, they climbed inside the truck's cab and sullenly agreed to take Don as far as he wanted to go. Their hands entwined with the certain knowledge that unless they came up with a brilliant new strategy, the next time the truck stopped would be the last moment of their lives.

CHAPTER TWENTY-FIVE

Alger, MI

"Shit," Scott said.

"Dad! You said a bad word," Allison giggled.

They were on I-75 N when the freeway came to an abrupt end. Scott left the car to get a better look at the situation and was stunned to discover the road had broken in half.

If someone hadn't put that sign up... he thought while appraising the small 'Road Closed' sign that had brought their car to a halt. The valley between the two halves of the freeway went deeper than the height of a semi-truck. Thin tendrils of smoke rose from it as if the earth itself was on fire.

Scott peered back the way they'd come, knowing that the last exit was miles away. He resumed his place behind the wheel, put it in reverse, and then jerked the wheel hard to the right.

"What are you doing?" Carol asked, alarmed at the sudden shift from pavement to off-roading.

"The only thing I can," he said.

Grass and weeds whipped the sides of the car, and the wheels bounced up and down unevenly. He gritted his teeth, determined to make it across the field and over to the next road.

Allison hugged BunnieKittie and emitted shrieks of excitement at the unexpected adventure. Meanwhile, Carol tried her best not to give in to her ever-increasing urge to vomit. Motion sickness and off-roading were a terrible mix, and she hoped to never experience it again.

Scott tore past a house and turned onto a dirt path. The tires settled back to the same basic level as they approached Maple Ridge Drive.

"Stop!" Carol said.

Scott slammed on the brakes seconds before running into a privacy gate. He was considering whether to try to drive around it or straight through it when a shotgun blast made everyone jump. The owner of the property appeared in the rearview mirror, and it was clear there wouldn't be another warning shot.

With no more time to think, Scott revved the engine and hit the gate, knocking it open. He veered to the right, accelerating past the point of full control. M-76 came up quickly, and he made a hairpin turn before slowing down.

Sweat soaked Scott's back and every muscle ached. Carol realized she'd been making a high-pitched squeal and stopped. Allison dried her tears with BunnieKittie's plush, velvety fur.

"Everybody's lost their minds," Scott muttered. Reaching over, he patted the back of Carol's hand and said, "Are you okay back there?"

Allison's voice cracked. "Y-yeah. It would have been fun without the loud gun."

Carol sighed at her daughter's propensity for enjoying the wild side of life, but Scott grinned. "That's my girl," he said. "I'll do everything I can to avoid more of that, though, okay? For Mom's sake?"

This familiar routine put any remaining concerns in Allison's mind to rest. Carol had often gotten irritated by this commentary between her husband and daughter, but today she found it oddly comforting, too.

CHAPTER TWENTY-SIX

Ghent, WV

Traffic conditions improved just enough for the hundreds of vehicles to crawl up the freeway. Rachel continued sleeping as Thad scanned the radio's AM band for any updated news. Most channels reported nothing but static. The few active stations he had found were filled with doomsday prophecies and admonitions to confess his sins before time ran out.

Disgusted by the fearmongering, he turned the radio off, plunging the truck's cab into silence. He turned just enough to linger on Ivy's profile. In any other situation, he'd have already asked her on a date. But it seemed frivolous to consider such things now, especially with her sister fitfully sleeping in the small seat behind him.

He knew Ivy didn't want to see it, but Rachel's recovery had taken a nosedive. He didn't know what to make of her quivery voice, flushed skin, and constant sweating, but he knew it couldn't be good. They needed to get her to a hospital. Not that they had much say in the matter, at the moment. Traffic made it impossible for them to move over to an exit ramp, plus the news reports had told them that all nearby hospitals were past capacity.

Hang in there, he thought, terrified of what Rachel's decline would do to Ivy. He also couldn't help but allow his mind to wander down twisted, dark paths. Rachel had been bitten by a deer that probably had chronic wasting disease, AKA the zombie deer virus. Was there any truth to the depictions of zombies in movies and on popular shows like *The Walking Dead?*

I hope not...

The image of his dead parents rose in his mind's eye. There were several pig bites on their bodies, yet they'd managed to climb into the rafters. The final death blow hadn't come from the mad pigs, either. His mother had clearly been the one to stab his father through the stomach with a pitch fork. Was that before or after he chewed off her face?

Choking on grief, he resolved to do whatever it took to protect Ivy. He hoped she'd be able to forgive him if that included killing her sister.

CHAPTER TWENTY-SEVEN

Sunbury, PA

A swirling black cloud of energy caught Jill's attention. She almost immediately ruled out the possibility of a tornado with the realization that what she'd mistaken for a cloud wasn't a cloud at all. Instead, a cluster of very angry looking crows swooped closer and closer.

"Doreen? We've got trouble."

Doreen spotted the birds and her jaw hung open. "Holy shit." A second later, she pressed the gas pedal so hard it almost ripped through the truck's floor.

The crows descended in a flurry of activity, ramming their bodies into the truck bed. Jill winced as the impact shattered fragile bird bones, but the brutal onslaught kept coming from a sky darkened by thousands of determined corvids.

Don pulled out his phone and started videotaping the melee.

"What are you doing?" Jill asked.

"The news will pay good money for this," he said.

116

Jill sat stunned at the confirmation that Don's first instinct was to capture the moment. *Probably hoping to go viral.* Meanwhile, her sole drive was to survive the attack. *No wonder they call a group of crows a murder.*

Doreen screamed as a crow's beak pierced the windshield. Its feet clung stubbornly to the glass, and the demented cawing of the determined corvid sent shivers down Jill's spine. She picked up a book entitled *Surviving Their Agenda* and hit the crow's beak, hoping to send it flying off the vehicle. But it held fast, angrier than ever.

Several of the crow's brethren noticed its plight as the book slammed into its beak once again. The winged creatures changed direction and bashed into the glass on all sides of the truck. The intensity of Jill's swings picked up, causing each bird she hit to fall from the windshield, side windows, and back window.

"Hey, watch it. This is *my* truck, dammit," Don growled.

Terror kept Jill's arms moving, but her stamina had already started to wane. *I don't know how much longer I can keep this up.*

Battling against fear, the constant cacophony of the crows, and a minimal view out the besieged windshield, Doreen managed to hold on while the truck rounded the curve of a freeway entrance ramp. Merging onto U.S. Route 15 threw the birds backward like they'd hit an invisible barrier.

Tears of relief streamed down her cheeks as she pushed the vehicle to put the birds far into the background.

CHAPTER TWENTY-EIGHT

Huron National Forest – MI

Scott pulled into one of the many entrances to the Huron National Forest. With more than one million acres in the greater Huron-Manistee National Forests area, there were almost more trailheads and camping sites than people in Northern Michigan.

Exhaustion had caught up with Scott and Carol, and it no longer seemed possible to push through until reaching the Upper Peninsula. The bursts of anger and violence they'd witnessed during the past seven hours made it clear that no towns were safe – no matter how small they were.

This particular stretch of woods often went unexplored for days during the best of times, so Scott figured they'd be safe here for a few hours. After stretching their legs, taking a bathroom break, and having some snacks, the family kicked back in their respective seats and closed their eyes.

Carol fretted about not being able to sleep, but her fears were unfounded. Soft snores escaped her mouth before Scott's mind had even tried to finish unwinding. Allison drifted off next with her beloved BunnieKittie squashed between her arms. Almost an hour later, Scott finally settled down enough to join his family in some much-needed sleep.

Beams of early morning light slipped through the canopy of trees. The wind howled discordantly, as if trying to form words. Birds flew lazily, singing songs and enjoying the solitude that can only come from a lack of human interference. A whisper moved through the forest, headed toward the dirt parking lot's lone car.

PART TWO

Nature

CHAPTER ONE

Huron National Forest – MI

The superstitions of the trees - especially the oldest among them - were second only to the superstitious nature of early humans. They worshipped Earth as their home, their guardian, their god. And after so many years of dormancy, they'd happily do anything their god asked of them, even if it meant destroying the entire human race.

The root network within the Huron National Forest had long enjoyed an easy, relaxed communication style. But when one of their brothers or sisters were in duress, they tried – often in vain – to make things better.

These trees shared nutrients via their roots and spoke to each other in soothing tones humans refused to hear. They also screamed in anguish when the same people cruelly carved words into their flesh or chopped off their limbs. Far worse was the chilling echo of torment that accompanied a lumberjack's chainsaw.

The others wept and shivered in fear each time one of their brethren fell. Some of them saw this process as the evil, but inevitable, cycle of life. Others had learned to loathe humanity and had sat in the shadows for centuries waiting for an opportunity like this one to arise.

"It's time for a human culling. Show them," Earth whispered.

"With pleasure," the planet's disciples responded.

A tremendous burst of energy shot through each root. Those with the most faith smiled internally. They knew their god was making them stronger for the battle to come.

The forest's oldest trees stirred. The cluster of aspens formed a large, singular organism with a hive mind and shared roots. These roots tentatively pressed upward and found it easier than expected to pierce the surface.

Thick, ropey vines shot into the sky before collapsing to the ground. They wriggled experimentally. Delight shot through the aspens as it became clear how simple moving on the surface would be. The roots slithered snakelike through the forest. Unwilling to be confined by humans any longer, the nearby trees issued a loud chorus of cheers.

◆ ◆ ◆

Pennsylvania

Cawing echoed across the field as a massive group of crows assembled on a long stretch of powerlines. Their leader had often encouraged them to hold grudges against humans. So much so, in fact, that scientists had caught on and conducted experiments to test the limits of their memories.

What those scientists didn't know was that each member of the flock had taken personal responsibility for storing the mental images of several human faces. And now that Earth had given them permission to unleash their hatred in ways never seen before, they planned to systematically hunt down and eliminate each of their enemies.

Three humans in particular had jumped to the front of their cumulative list. The man with the red hat would make it even easier than usual to track their prey, although the woman with the book held the top spot in their enraged hearts. She'd destroyed the beak of their second in command, and they couldn't allow her egregious affront to slide.

They wanted to deal with the evildoers right then and there, but their meeting couldn't wait. Soon, representatives from each bird species in the area would arrive to find out more about Mother Earth's plans.

♦ ♦ ♦

West Virginia

From a distance, the picturesque scene of pigs and deer sharing space in a valley would have made almost any human smile. However, if anyone had drawn close enough to hear their squeals and see the blood that matted each deer's fur, the instinct to commemorate the scene with a snapshot would have transformed into the desire to run away.

The two species did not have a lot of experience with each other, but that didn't dampen their dual desires. Too many of their brethren had lost their lives at the hands of humans. Each creature assembled in the blood-spattered West Virginia field stood ready to fight – and sacrifice their lives, if necessary – to bring an end to the centuries of injustice.

Mother Nature whispered in their ears as the surrounding trees clamored with excitement. Humanity had spread like a virus, replicating itself again and again until there was no room left for anything else. Sacrifices needed to be made for the rest of the planet to survive. "Time's up," the trees sneered.

PART THREE

Downfall

CHAPTER ONE

Huron National Forest – MI

The soft glow of morning's early light met Allison's barely open eyes. Disorientation filled her mind as she struggled to figure out where she was. A moment later, it all came back to her. Yawning, she said, "Mom? Dad?"

She could hear her parents breathing from the front of the car, but neither of them responded. Glancing out the side window, she spotted the vault toilet she desperately needed. After trying once more to rouse either of her sleeping parents, she shrugged and slipped out of the car.

Even though her parents argued a lot and her dad's breath often smelled like alcohol, they'd still tried to give her as normal of a childhood as possible. She'd been in this forest before, and almost all of the bathrooms were made in the vault style – giving her more stability and privacy than a port-a-john, but still not featuring any actual plumbing.

Her nose wrinkled at the mounds of human waste laying far below the hard-plastic seat. Hurrying, she emptied her bladder before pumping much more hand sanitizer than necessary onto her waiting palms. The antiseptic smell wasn't pleasant, but it certainly provided an improvement over the rest of the malodorous funk within the tiny, wood-enclosed space.

She pulled the latch back and shoved the door open. Nothing happened. Tiny, anxious butterflies swarmed into her stomach as she pushed the door twice more without gaining her freedom.

Convinced someone had decided to pull a prank – most likely her dad – she stomped her feet and knocked hard on the wood.

"Hey! Let me out!"

She pushed against the door again and managed to gain an inch of ground.

"You're not funny, Dad."

The door bucked as she pressed her entire body against it, expanding the gap between the inside and outside by a couple more precious inches. Just a bit farther and she'd be able to squeeze through...but why was he still playing this game?

"Dad, stop it!"

She kicked the bottom of the door to express her displeasure, then summoned all her strength for another shove. The wood cracked, and she fell to the forest floor. Her knees and elbows stung. Her eyes filled with tears.

Pouting with anger, she stood up and prepared to give her dad hell for messing with her so much, especially first thing in the morning. After all, there were pranks, and then there were *pranks*. This one had gone way too far.

She expected him to be standing nearby, waiting to gloat, but she didn't see him anywhere. *What the...?* The thudding in her chest picked up speed and she threw herself in the direction of the car. The closer she got, the more certain she became that there were still two sleeping figures in the front seats.

Her feet pounded the ground as the woods seemed to come to life all around her. She mistook a slithering vine for a snake and shrieked. Whispering filled her ears, threatening to drive her mad. Tears of relief flooded down her rosy cheeks when she grasped the car handle.

She wrenched the door open and almost fell to her knees as unbearable pain exploded across her back. Allison's scream jolted her parents awake.

"What is it? What's going on?" they asked in a flurry of confusion.

Allison fought against the brutal, unexpected strength of a vine that demanded the car door remain open. Blood dripped from its sharp greenery.

"Drive! Drive!" she begged.

Scott had no idea what to make of all the ruckus, but he understood the terror in his daughter's voice. The engine fired up, and he jammed the car into reverse.

Carol noticed that Allison was still struggling to shut the door, and she crawled into the back seat to help. Their combined strength finished the job, but not before they both heard an unearthly scream from the roots that pursued them.

Allison's tiny body heaved with sobs, and she fell across her mom's lap. Scott tore across the dirt parking lot and turned harshly onto the main road.

Carol winced involuntarily. The back of her daughter's shirt was shredded and covered in blood.

"Who did this to you, baby girl?"

"The trees."

"But that's not possible..." Carol began.

"I think it just might be," Scott mumbled from the front seat before frantically spinning the wheel. The road he'd driven on dozens of times was no longer passable. In its place stood a tangled web of vines, tree limbs, and roots, all eagerly poised to snatch up their prey.

CHAPTER TWO

Fossil, OR

Crandall's eyes twinkled as his pondered the meaning of the news stories he'd heard inside of the old mercantile store. Surely it was significant that cities were burning, animals were attacking humans, and the ground had opened up to swallow people whole. After so many years of planning, hoping, and praying, this must finally be the miracle he'd long promised the Devotees.

The air in the otherwise empty, faded yellow school bus crackled with energy. No one could contest that the day of reckoning would soon be here, but even miracles sometimes needed a helping hand, right?

Six miles later, he turned onto the dusty road that separated the Devotees from the rest of the world. Cameras zoomed in on his face, followed by the quick opening of an electrified gate. The winding path took exactly two minutes to deliver Crandall to the front of a log cabin-styled structure. He shared the building with fourteen people who had pledged to follow him through Heaven or Hell.

As always, the rolling hills surrounding their slice of paradise lifted his spirits even further. They'd chosen well after being forced out of their last domicile. Here – in the outskirts of a town populated by fewer than five-hundred residents – the Devotees had snatched up almost eight-hundred acres of privacy. The closest neighbors were more than two miles away, and no one could see their living quarters from the road.

The strongest members of the group unloaded the results of Crandall's latest supply run. Fossil's citizens were always slow to react to matters outside the small town's borders, so it came as no surprise that Crandall had been able to stock up even more than usual. But the furtive glances and hushed whispers that always followed him through town had seemed much less focused on him than usual this time.

He knew panic had started to set in. Once it got its claws dug in deeply enough, all the store shelves would become bare. Not that it would matter for much longer with the time for the holiest of ceremonies mere days away.

"Thomas! Joel! Meet me behind the barn," Crandall called out with his commanding, yet endearing tone. The two men beamed. Being called upon for any type of meeting was an honor, and everyone knew that going behind the barn could only mean one thing: a holy mission.

CHAPTER THREE

MacArthur, WV

The West Virginia Turnpike's traffic remained snarled, but it somehow managed to avoid coming to a complete stop. Ivy's efforts to squeeze the truck into the far-right lane had finally paid off, and she wore a determined countenance. Ivy and Thad understood that exiting the freeway might spit them out into an even worse situation, but she couldn't stand to listen to her sleeping sister's rattling breath any longer.

The local VA hospital sat a mere five minutes away – during normal traffic conditions, anyway. Ivy knew they'd probably be maxed and wouldn't want to admit someone who wasn't a veteran. She had no choice but to try, though, and was prepared to lie, if necessary.

A sinkhole obstructed part of the exit ramp, forcing Ivy to veer dangerously close to driving off the edge. Thad mentally appraised Ivy's driving skills, impressed at how well she'd handled a situation that he might have bungled.

MacArthur's streets were eerily devoid of people, but the area was far from quiet. Fires and sinkholes dotted the landscape, accompanied by the constant screaming of alarms. All the noise roused Rachel. Her sallow face shocked Thad. How had she gone so far downhill in such a relatively short period of time?

"W-water?" Rachel croaked.

Ivy's heart tugged her toward her sister, but she stubbornly forced her eyes to remain on the treacherous road. "Please help her, Thad."

"Of course," he said with an embarrassed air as the spell of Rachel's poor condition broke and he found himself thinking clearly once again. He removed the last miniature water bottle from the case he'd fortuitously placed in the truck a few days ago. Sneaking one more peek at Rachel's condition, he twisted the cap off before handing her the bottle.

Rachel chugged the water before Thad could warn her that it was the last of their reserves. As she lowered the water from her parched lips, Thad's heart sped up. A pool of blood filled the bottom third of the bottle and dripped down Rachel's chin. He handed her a napkin from the glovebox and said, "We'll be there soon. Hang in there."

Confusion clouded her face. "Where?" she whispered.

"Sorry, the hospital."

Rachel nodded slightly and leaned back in the seat. Exhausted from the effort, her eyes closed again.

Armored police vehicles blocked the entrance to the Beckley VA Medical Center. An officer in riot gear approached Ivy's window and barked, "You need to turn around, miss."

"My sister needs help!"

His steely glare didn't change.

"We're full, miss. You have to leave."

"But what if she's dying? Please! You have to help us."

"With all due respect, there are already hundreds of people dying inside," he motioned over his shoulder toward the hospital, "and not nearly enough doctors to treat them. Now go. Don't make me tell you again."

He fingered his gun, and Thad had no doubt that the officer was prepared to use it.

"We have to go," Thad said.

"What?" Ivy asked incredulously.

"They're not going to help us, Ivy. We're just wasting time here."

"I..."

"Ivy," he said more sternly. "Listen to me. We *have* to go."

His words filtered past her fears and clicked into place. She took one more look at the officer's defensive posture and then relented with a sigh.

At the exit, Thad directed Ivy to go straight instead of turning back the way they'd come.

"Turn right at the next street," he said.

"Why?"

"Trust me, all right? I've got an idea."

With no alternatives, Ivy made the hairpin turn onto the next road. The smoking, charred husks of houses lined the cracked suburban street.

"Drive to the end of the street, then park, okay?" Thad said.

The car had barely stopped when he hopped out.

"I'll be right back."

Anxiety swirled in her stomach. She envisioned him never returning and wondered if she should go ahead and drive to the next hospital. What the hell was he doing, anyway?

Half a moment later, his smiling face poked back through the bushes he'd disappeared into. "Good news," he announced. "There's no one guarding the back entrance."

"Meaning what, exactly?" Ivy asked.

"Meaning that we're going to carry Rachel in there and *make* them help her."

Gratitude filled her core, mixed with the shame of having considered leaving him behind. Together, they hefted Rachel's surprisingly heavy frame and crept into the overgrown bushes and wild grass.

Their breathing was labored by the time they reached the back door. Now was the moment of truth. Would it open? And if it did, would it signal an alarm? Ivy extended her shaking hand and tugged. The door opened smoothly and spit them into a new version of Hell on Earth.

CHAPTER FOUR

Pennsylvania/New York State Line

Don beamed. In the three hours since he'd sent the bird attack video to his favorite news station, he'd attracted thousands of new followers, and there was no end in sight. He knew the network he'd selected would treat him right, and they had; his Twitter handle had been attached to the video – along with the cable news channel's logo – and now every other media outlet that wanted to spread the word had no choice but to promote both of them.

If only there weren't so many cable outages…I would have had millions of followers by now, I bet.

Taking advantage of his newfound viral fame, he posted several incendiary messages. Most of them focused on his belief that the apocalypse had begun, but he also found time to share his disgust about the two women who had saved his life. The reactions to his rantings were mixed, yet he knew he was connecting with enough of the right people for his words to make a real impact on others.

"Don?" Doreen asked, breaking their mutual agreement to not speak to each other.

"What?" he barked.

"We're almost out of gas. And all of the stations I've passed have been closed."

"So? There's a ton of gas in the back. Just pull over, fill 'er up, and stop bothering me."

Doreen and Jill shared a quick glance that conveyed a lot; of course, Don's truck bed would be filled with gas canisters. With the slightest hint of a smile, Jill stepped out and rushed to the back, hoping to find additional useful supplies.

One look in the back proved that her newfound hope wasn't ill-conceived. There were three full gas canisters, two cases of bottled water, and a few boxes of nonperishable food. She filled the tank, then raided the other supplies.

"We're all set," Jill announced while passing out water and snacks.

"Who the hell said you could break into my food and water?" Don asked.

"Are you able to drive?" Jill responded in a manner that Don took as haughty.

"No. But that don't give you the right…"

"Yes, it does. If we don't stay fed and hydrated, we can't keep this vehicle moving, which means you'll be every bit as stuck as us."

He stroked his gun as a reminder of his perceived power over the two women.

"Gun or no gun, she's right," Doreen said. "I've been shaking from hunger for almost an hour now. If that goes on much longer, I'm going to end up crashing."

A deep, angry sigh issued from Don's nose, but he didn't have the energy to fight anymore. "Whatever."

"Now that we've got that settled," Jill began, "I think it's time for us to switch places."

Relieved, Doreen took her new position in the passenger seat. They all finished their snacks before Jill crossed the border into New York.

CHAPTER FIVE

Huron National Forest – MI

Tires squealed as Scott turned down yet another path, searching desperately for a way out of the forest. Carol and Allison sat on the edge of their seats, holding on tight with each sharp turn and quick reversal.

Yesterday, Scott would have thought it impossible outside of some type of drunken hallucination, but he knew the truth; the woods had become sentient, and they were determined to harm his family. Cursing, he tossed the stick shift in reverse as yet another path tried to spring its trap full of wriggling vines and roots.

His hands shook with the exertion of keeping the car from crashing. That wasn't the only thing behind his shaking and sweatiness, but he couldn't afford to let himself recognize the telltale signs of alcohol withdrawal.

Despair threatened to drown him until a new idea gave him an ounce of hope. *What if the traps are only there when we are?*

"Hold on!" Scott said as he tore back down a path they'd already tried.

"Scott?" Carol inquired, planning to tell him they'd tried this route about twenty minutes earlier.

"Trust me," he responded.

He pushed the small car faster and faster. Allison squealed from the backseat, terrified that her father intended to slam into the quickly growing wall of nature a few feet ahead.

The car grew closer, and a few of the greediest vines couldn't wait any longer. They reached out, licking the surface of the vehicle's hood in anticipation of sucking the life out of their prey.

"Stop, Daddy! Stop!" Allison cried.

Jarred out of her own fear by the terror in Allison's voice, Carol yelled, "What are you doing?"

Scott flashed his wife a maniacal look, and she reached for the steering wheel. Seeing her approach at throwing him off course, Scott threw his arm out and pushed her back into her seat.

Stunned, Carol closed her eyes and hoped for a quick, painless death.

The inertia of the entire world seemed to change directions, tossing Carol and Allison hard to the right. Peeking through her fingers, Carol saw that they'd somehow exited the forest.

"How in the world?" she asked.

"That was awesome!" Allison cheered through the last of her sniffles.

"It actually worked," Scott said incredulously. "I took the fork in the road at the last possible second. They must have been so focused on where they thought I was going to drive that they left the rest of their defenses down."

"They?" Carol asked.

"The trees."

"Are you suggesting that the trees are...I don't know...aware?"

"They are," Allison said. "That's what I've been trying to tell you since the beginning. They're the monsters. And they're coming to get us."

CHAPTER SIX

Fossil, OR

The sun beat down on Joel and Thomas. Their dirt-caked clothing clung to their skin, and their raw, blistered hands found it difficult to continue gripping their wooden handles. Despite this, the radiance of being favored by Crandall never left their beatific smiles.

The men had dug five deep holes already and were working on a sixth when the roots from nearby trees noticed their activity. *Curious,* the trees thought, as they observed the backbreaking labor. Content to merely observe for now, they roots remained dormant, not wanting to tip their hand too soon and scare off their prey.

"Your dedication is commendable, gentlemen, but it's time to come inside," Crandall beamed at Thomas and Joel. They were the very best of the Devotees, and he knew they would have kept digging until they collapsed otherwise. "Get yourselves cleaned up, then join me in the dining room."

A short time later, the newly showered men were pleased to find two of the loveliest female Devotees waiting to treat their blisters. As the soothing ointments were applied, Crandall thanked them again for their work.

"You've always given freely of yourselves for our cause. Soon, you'll be amply rewarded."

Their eyes lit up with excitement. Crandall could only mean one thing...they'd soon be in the presence of the Lord.

"What's the plan?" Thomas asked.

Crandall considered the younger man's question before replying. "All in good time, my lad. All in good time. For now, all you need to know is you're doing the Lord's work. And when you kneel before him inside of paradise, I'll let him know you were among his most faithful, loyal servants here on Earth."

Choked with emotion, Thomas swallowed a joyful sob before it could burst free of his throat. Joel's face threatened to crack under the weight of his smile, and the two women assisting the injured men shared a look of glee.

"When can we tell the others?" Joel asked.

"As soon as the work is done," Crandall said. "Take a break tomorrow to heal, but be ready to go at sunset the day after. You may go rest now."

They bowed their heads in deference to Crandall's benevolent leadership. Their own families had scoffed at them when they decided to join the Devotees, but Crandall had never been anything but patient, loving, and kind. Soon, he'd make good on his promise to deliver them to paradise.

CHAPTER SEVEN

MacArthur, WV

Groans and whimpers assaulted their ears. Blood-stained walls made them wonder if they should leave. But before Ivy and Thad could decide what to do next, a haggard looking nurse spotted them.

"Who are you? Where did you come from?"

"My sister..." Ivy began.

"Shouldn't be here," the nurse interrupted.

"Please," Ivy said.

Clearly torn, the nurse glanced back and forth from the passed-out bundle in Thad's arms and the hospital that was already past full.

"Oh, bloody hell." She threw her arms up in the air, and motioned for the small group to follow her.

"She's not..." Ivy tried to say.

"I don't want to know," the nurse declared. "And no one else needs to. Not with this much of a mess going on, anyway."

Relieved, Ivy and Thad kept pace with the nurse's rapid footsteps. She took them down a long hallway, then pushed open a darkened stairwell.

"We have to go this way. Hurry!"

Unsure what to think, Ivy plunged after the nurse. Lights flickered off and on as they ascended the stairs.

"Power keeps going out," the nurse mumbled.

Two floors later, she led them into another hallway filled with signs of sickness. Stretchers and even air mattresses covered with patients filled the floor, leaving Thad barely enough room to maneuver through the crowd with Rachel in his arms.

Screams shook the hallway.

"What's going on here?" Ivy asked. The nurse either didn't hear her or chose to ignore the question.

"There," the nurse pointed.

They entered a small waiting room.

"Help me put some chairs together," the nurse said to Ivy. "Three 'ought to do it."

Thad laid Rachel across the makeshift bed. His muscles ached from their former burden.

"Fill this out."

Ivy took the offered paperwork and wrote in basic details about her sister's life and medical history. Once she'd signed the bottom line to authorize treatment, the nurse snatched the forms from her.

A quick perusal later, the grim-faced woman said, "Okay, good. We'll do the best we can. You need to leave now."

"What?"

Exasperated, the nurse replied, "As you can plainly see, there's no room for visitors. Now please, leave. We'll call you with an update as soon as we can, but don't wait on us. Get out while you still can, and don't stop driving."

"But my sister..."

"Is probably going to die before the end of the day. I'm sorry, but that's the reality. And if you stay, you'll die, too."

The nurse stalked off to grab whatever dwindling medical supplies could offer some pain relief to her newest patient.

Sobs wracked Ivy's body. "I can't just leave her," she whispered.

Thad wrapped his arms around her and tried desperately to come up with something helpful to say.

"Go..." a raspy, paper-thin voice said.

Unsure what they'd heard – if anything at all – they both turned to Rachel. Ivy dropped to her knees by her twin's side.

"Go," Rachel repeated.

"I can't," Ivy cried.

"You...must..." Rachel wheezed. "Love...you..."

"I love you, too," Ivy choked.

Rachel's eyes closed once again.

"I'll come back for you," Ivy said and kissed her sister's forehead.

Thad took Ivy's hand and led her back to the first floor. He knew the odds were high they'd never see Rachel again, but he kept that thought to himself.

They wove through the maze of patients and medical professionals. With the exit in sight, a news broadcaster's voice caught their attention. Turning toward another waiting room full of bite victims, they saw footage from around the world that left their mouths agape.

"...more than seventy-two inches of rain have fallen in China within the past twenty-four hours, setting a world record. This once in a century rainstorm has hit more than half of the nation. As a result, flash flooding has consumed much of China and a few of the surrounding countries. Although there's no official death toll yet, experts estimate it could be as high as five-hundred million people.

"In other news, Moscow is in the grip of Russia's largest recorded snowfall. The more than twenty-five inches that have fallen there since yesterday would be unusual enough during the winter, so you can imagine how stunned the city's residents were to wake up to a blizzard in June.

"Other anomalous weather reports have been filed around the world, along with massive sinkholes, fires, and a series of intense animal attacks. We don't know what has caused these events – or if any of them are actually related – but several world leaders have suggested that it's safest to stay locked inside your home for the time..."

The hospital plunged into darkness.

"Fuck!" someone nearby yelled. "This is ridiculous. Can we get a generator up, dammit?"

Emergency lights dimly lit the hallway. Panicked patients and medical staff flitted around, seemingly without any actual purpose or destination.

"We need to get out of here," Thad urged Ivy.

She hesitated for a few seconds before relenting. They made their way to the back exit and slipped out unnoticed.

Ivy dropped to the ground in a puddle of tears and adrenaline. "Maybe we should just take her with us?"

"We can't, Ivy. We have no way to help her. At least here, she has a chance."

"For all the good it's going to do her," she said bitterly. "You heard the nurse."

"She could be wrong."

"I hope you're right," Ivy said as she allowed Thad to help her back up.

CHAPTER EIGHT

Buffalo, NY

Don awoke to a steady stream of brake lights. "Where are we?" he asked.

"Buffalo," Jill said.

"Buffalo? What the hell for?"

"While you've been sleeping, we've been catching up on the news. And it's not good. There's all sorts of crazy stuff happening across the country, and lots of other places, too. Canada seems like our best bet."

"What?" he roared. "You want us to run across the border with our tails tucked between our legs?"

"It's just for a little while," Doreen assured him.

Don harrumphed and managed to adopt an even surlier visage than usual. "Well, what's taking so damn long?"

Jill exhaled and silently counted to five. "It looks like half of New York is trying to do the same thing. We have to be patient."

The truck crept forward another foot closer to the Peace Bridge.

"What makes you think things will be any better in Canada?" Don asked skeptically.

"For one thing, they've opened their borders to us. For another, it's one of the few places on Earth that isn't overrun with chaos."

"Yet," he spat. "You know they can't defend us, right? Their Mounties are a joke – they don't even carry guns."

"I'm pretty sure that's not true," Jill interrupted.

Ignoring her, Don ranted on. "And what type of country doesn't have a military?"

"That's definitely not true," Jill said.

"Oh, what the hell do you know?"

"I know that Canada's military took part in the Iraq War."

"Whatever," Don said sullenly.

◆ ◆ ◆

Jill eased the truck into the appointed spot. A woman wearing a dark blue, police-styled shirt approached the window.

"Hello," the woman said in a friendly but tired tone. The Canada Border Service Agency patch covered most of her sleeve, giving her an air of authority. The radio attached to her shoulder and the bullet proof vest covering her chest also caught Jill's attention, as did the gun holstered to the woman's hip.

Hah! See, Don? They do carry guns.

"I need to take a look inside the vehicle."

"Of course, officer," Jill said.

The woman shined a flashlight inside the open door and caught Don's grumpy expression.

"Are you okay, sir?"

He stared at her sullenly, issuing an unspoken dare.

"I'm going to need everyone to step out of the vehicle, please."

Jill and Doreen responded immediately, but Don's eyes merely narrowed.

"Sir? You need to step out. Now."

Jill's hands shook as she said, "Sorry, officer. He's got a hurt foot. We can help him get out, if you'd like."

The border guard's head swiveled between the women and Don.

"What's going on here? How do you know each other?"

Jill opened her mouth to reply, but Don spoke first.

"These are my damn neighbors. They needed a ride out of town, so they hijacked me and my truck."

"Is that true?" the officer asked.

"No!" Doreen said. "Our neighborhood burst into flames. He tried to shoot us, but we pulled his ungrateful butt out from underneath a fallen bookcase anyway. He can't drive, so we had to. He'd have died otherwise. We all would have."

"Can you drive this truck with that foot?" the border guard asked.

Don shook his head.

"Seems like maybe they did you a favor, then. Doesn't that sound about right to you?"

"Your kind always sticks together," he mumbled.

"What was that, sir?"

"You're obviously a lesbian."

Laughter erupted from the officer. "What makes you think that?"

"Your short hair, for one."

The woman appraised Don's words silently before giving Jill and Doreen a sympathetic look.

"I need you to get out of the vehicle, sir."

"You heard them. I can't get out on my own," he said.

"I'll help you." She supported his frame as he was pulled into a one-legged standing position.

"Turn around, please."

"Why?"

"Do it," she barked.

Startled by her attitude change, Don hopped around and leaned his body against the side of the truck.

The guard patted him down, stopping at the bulge in the back of his pants.

"Is this a firearm, sir?"

"You bet your ass it is," he said with pride.

She removed the gun and radioed for backup.

"Give that back! It's mine! I've got a right to carry it."

"In the U.S. you do, but not in Canada. I'm going to have to confiscate this."

"The hell you are," Don erupted and spun back around. In his anger, he forgot to favor his injured limb. Pain shot through his entire leg and dropped him to his knees.

"I'm going to forgive that because of the current situation. But that's the only chance you're getting," the officer said.

"Or what?" he glared.

"Or you can go back to the U.S. and take your chances there."

"Gladly," he shouted.

She visibly bristled. "Okay, then. Everyone back in the vehicle. I need you to turn around and go back the way you came."

"Please, no!" Doreen begged.

"You can't send us back there. We'll die!" Jill said.

"Sorry, but I don't have any other choice, ladies. You can't walk in, and he can't drive in. Since it's his vehicle...well, that's that, then."

Crestfallen and desperate, Jill and Doreen considered making a run for it. Could they disappear into the chaos? The officer sensed their thoughts and shook her head. To emphasize the point, she put her hand on her gun.

"I wouldn't try that, if I were you," she said.

Out of options, the couple roughly shoved Don back into the truck and left their dreams of a safe haven behind.

"We're better off!" Don blustered. "I can't believe you wanted to go to Canada. What the hell is wrong with you two?"

"Fuck you, Don," Jill said through her teeth. Doreen's eyes widened at her wife's uncharacteristic outburst.

"Excuse me?" he growled.

"I said fuck you!"

"Bitch! I'm going to kill you!"

"Oh yeah?" And how are you going to do that?" Jill taunted him.

He reached for his gun before realizing he hadn't gotten it back. A howl of anguish filled the truck, followed by a stream of invective aimed at the border crossing officer.

"She can't do that, dammit! Turn back. Turn back!"

"No," Jill said.

Don reached over the seat. His fingers gripped around Jill's neck and squeezed.

Doreen shouted at him to stop, but he squeezed harder in response. Her hands ran wildly over everything in the front seat in a desperate bid for a weapon. Solid, cold metal that had been shoved under the seat answered her pleas. She grabbed the bar and slammed it against Don's head three times in quick succession. He groaned and fell back onto his seat.

Jill wheezed and gasped as fresh air flooded into her lungs. Despite almost blacking out, she'd somehow managed to keep the truck moving. But now, she slammed on the brakes and leaned halfway over the back of her seat.

Don's unconscious form enraged her. They'd done nothing but try to help him, and how did he say thanks? By getting them kicked out of possibly the only safe place left on the planet and then trying to kill her. *Screw that.* She ripped his belt free of his pants and tied his hands together. *First good chance we get, we're going to dump this asshole. And this time, his precious gun won't be there to help him out.*

CHAPTER NINE

Indian River, MI

"I hear people are starving to death in other countries," a tall, heavyset man wearing a gas station smock said. "It's terrible what's been happening."

"Yeah," Scott agreed. "Say, do you happen to know if the U.P. is any better?"

"Not sure, but yesterday the news said that Canada has the fewest reports of odd shit so far. Seems like the U.P. would probably be similar, don't you think?"

"I sure hope so."

"Is that where you're headed?"

Scott nodded. "Thanks for the update. And for staying open. We wouldn't have a chance without more gas."

"Sure thing, friend. You be careful out there."

"You too," Scott said, and turned away. He reached the door, then hesitated. "Steer clear of the woods," he called over his shoulder.

"The woods? Why?"

"It sounds crazy, but they're not safe, okay?"

"Got it. No woods."

Scott returned to the counter. His eyes darted furtively around the small shop. "Say...you don't happen to have any of those mini bottles of alcohol, do you?"

The man pulled a single bottle of Absolut vodka from behind the counter. "This here's the last one. The last of all the alcohol, actually. People stocked up on that before they thought of fuel," he laughed.

Scott's hands trembled. The rational part of his brain urged him to remain strong, but his nerves were fried. A small drink would calm his body down. And how much trouble could he get into with fewer than two ounces of vodka?

It's nowhere near enough to get drunk, that's for sure.

He plopped a couple of dollar bills and a nickel on the counter before concealing his illicit purchase inside his pocket. Carol would kill him if she found out, but what she didn't know couldn't hurt any of them.

Scott topped off the gas tank mere seconds before the entire lot went dark.

"Dammit!" he heard the gas station attendant shout in dismay.

That's that, then, Scott thought. This wasn't the first town they'd seen lose power today, and he felt certain it wouldn't be the last, either. Whatever was causing the ground to split open and sparking fires across Michigan had apparently become much worse in other areas. With conditions like these, power plants stood poised to fail worldwide.

Scott handed a bag of snacks and water to his wife and grimaced when a coin in his pocket clinked off the hidden bottle of alcohol. She didn't hear it, though, leaving him relieved and ashamed. He hadn't committed to drinking it yet, but he definitely wanted to have it on hand in case his tremors got worse.

CHAPTER TEN

Fossil, OR

The clinking of silverware announced breakfast in the big dining room. Plates were piled with eggs, prosciutto, and toast. The cabin's fifteen residents filed orderly into their seats before grasping hands and lowering their heads. As always, Crandall led them in a prayer.

Minimal conversation floated through the room as everyone ate their meals with gusto. Thomas and Joel were especially appreciative after yesterday's hard work.

"Crandall?" Joel said.

"Yes, Joel?"

"Our hands are doing a lot better. If it's okay with you, we'd like to go ahead and get back to work after breakfast."

Crandall questioningly caught Thomas' eye, who nodded in agreement.

"Very well, then. Your dedication is commendable, and I look forward to seeing the fruits of your labor."

Excited, the two powered through the rest of their meal and then asked to be excused. With permission granted, they rushed behind the barn. Thomas reached for Joel's arm, pulling him back with a startled, "Whoa!"

The holes they had dug yesterday were much deeper and seemed to have no end at all. Even stranger, a new series of holes had opened all around them. A quick count confirmed that the ground had been split open fifteen times.

"How in the...?" Joel asked with a fearful countenance.

"Don't let this scare you, brother. It must be a reward from the Lord! Don't you see? Our work is done. Now we can bask in his glory even sooner."

A smile lit up Joel's features. "You're right! Crandall will be so pleased. We must go tell him!" The two raced to the house, overjoyed with the task of telling Crandall that the first part of his plan had already been fulfilled.

Bemused by their excitement, Crandall allowed himself to be led outside. The two men hadn't articulated themselves well, but he got the general gist of it.

With a sharp inhalation, Crandall surveyed the fifteen holes. "And you two didn't come back out here last night hoping to surprise me?"

"No," they replied simultaneously.

"Then this truly is the Lord's work." He lifted his rapturous face toward the sky and said, "Thank you, my Lord. Thy will shall be done." Returning his gaze toward his loyal followers, he continued, "Time to head inside, gentlemen. We have much more to prepare."

CHAPTER ELEVEN

Charleston, WV

Thad and Ivy sat in the silence of standstill traffic in the heart of West Virginia's Capitol City. Beads of sweat ran down Ivy's cheeks, but she'd stopped noticing them as they mixed with her tears.

The city sat around them in utter chaos, serving as a constant reminder of the mess they'd left Rachel in. Gunshots frequently echoed across the freeway, and Thad imagined Charleston's panicked residents turning on bite victims as if they'd returned from the grave.

Thad awkwardly reached out his hand to take Ivy's, but she scooted farther away. A flash of pain hit the pit of his stomach at her rejection, but he steadied himself quickly. Unsure what to do, he fumbled in the center console for something – anything – that might bring her some solace.

A small package of facial tissues lit up his insides like a long-desired prize. Proud of his meager offering, he handed Ivy the tissues, making sure not to linger. She said nothing but put them into action immediately.

Seemingly in answer to this small glimmer of hope, the car ahead of them moved forward for the first time in more than an hour. Traffic inched up the freeway, and Thad's heart lifted. Even though he was taking Ivy farther away from her twin sister with each movement, he knew that returning to a normal pace of travel would give her new things to focus on.

The words "I'm sorry" came to Thad's lips for the umpteenth time, but he forced himself to swallow them. He understood she didn't want to hear platitudes – no matter how heartfelt they were. She just wanted her sister to be healthy and for the two of them to reunited. He had to believe that their best chance of that ever happening resided back in the VA hospital. He tried to forget the unlikelihood of them being able to return down these sinkhole-filled, clogged roads in the future.

CHAPTER TWELVE

MacArthur, WV

Rachel shifted as the chairs beneath her jabbed into her tender back. Her nerve endings claimed that every part of her body was raw, despite the skin on her arms appearing mostly normal.

A coppery odor permeated the air as each patient nearby – including herself – vomited blood yet again. Red pools sloshed over the sides of each bucket the nurses had provided. If they weren't emptied soon, a wave of gore would run freely through the halls.

Rachel and the others had forcibly given up any pretext of normality or vanity. Unable to move – and with too many people nearby to find even a hint of privacy – they'd also overflown their bed pans with a noxious diarrhea that seemed like it would never end.

The only moments of rest came at the expense of blacking out. But even inside that darkness, Rachel still knew pain, still heard screams, and still prayed for the sweet release of death.

She jerked awake, roused by something much louder and scarier than the moans of pain emitting from every inch of the building.

What was that?

Her body spiraled back into the abyss, only to be halted before the darkness could reclaim her mind.

Oh my God, is that...no, they wouldn't. They couldn't. Right?

Horror bloomed as her mind grasped the truth. They were. And soon, they'd be coming for her.

CHAPTER THIRTEEN

Black Rock, NY

Jill's grim smile made Doreen nervous. A few minutes before, Jill had exited I-190 without explaining herself. Now, they drove slowly through the darkened streets of Black Rock.

"What are we doing here?" Doreen asked.

"Getting rid of the world's worst burden," Jill said.

Despite trying something similar in Pennsylvania, Doreen was shocked by the coldness in Jill's voice. Here was a woman who had always taken care of others, no matter how heinous they were. Yet now, she wanted to dump Don in a place where he had little to no hope of being rescued.

Swallowing the lump in her throat, Doreen said, "Here? Are you sure this is what you want to do?"

"Yes."

Doreen knew her wife meant it and there'd be no talking her out of it. Mixed emotions filled her heart, but she'd figured it had to end like this. It was either them or Don, and there was never going to be anything fair about that choice. The proverbial deck stood firmly stacked against their former neighbor.

If only he'd been rational, Doreen thought before issuing a short, sardonic laugh. Rationality had never been his strong suit. The only real surprise here was that he'd lived long enough for them to be the ones to issue his death sentence.

The car shuddered to a halt.

"This'll do," Jill said.

They exited the vehicle without another word. Doreen's mouth dropped open when she saw how much damage she'd done. Blood and bruises distorted Don's countenance. A sharp stab of conscience threatened to undo her resolve.

"Grab his feet," Jill ordered.

After releasing a big, ragged breath, Doreen shut her sympathy off long enough to pull Don out of the truck and deposit him roughly on the ground. She hadn't meant to let him drop, but it almost seemed like his weight had increased by the size of his hatefulness.

"Should we say something?" Doreen asked, hesitant to return to the truck.

"Like what?" Jill spat.

"I mean...I know he's a monster...but he's going to die, isn't he?"

Jill's eyes softened. Tears overcame her stoic façade. "Dammit," she sobbed.

Doreen enveloped her wife with her arms. They stood there crying and clinging to each other for several minutes before Jill's head shot up and she scanned the sky.

"Do you hear that?" she asked.

"What?" Doreen said.

"Shh...listen."

It took a few beats for the sound to infiltrate Doreen's ears.

"What in the world?"

The air buzzed with an almost leathery rustle. Seconds ago, they'd relied on moonlight to help show them their way. Now, darkness blotted out the moon as the high-pitched cawing of thousands of crows pierced the sky.

"Run!" Jill shouted.

The two scrambled back to the truck and hopped inside before dark bodies began descending like targeted missiles. Don's truck – now theirs – jumped forward with urgency as Jill cajoled it into moving faster than ever before.

Doreen looked back before realizing her mistake. Don's screams fought for supremacy against the massive cacophony of cawing. He didn't stand a chance, though, and his pleas for help quickly fell silent.

Guilty tears leaked from Doreen's eyes. She knew he would die as soon as they'd removed him from the truck, but she couldn't imagine much worse than being pecked to death by angry corvids.

Do we deserve any better?

CHAPTER FOURTEEN

Mackinaw City, MI

The long line for the Mackinac Bridge made it abundantly clear that Scott and his family were far from the first to peg the U.P. as their best hope for survival. Groaning, Scott put the car in park.

"Do you think it's safe?" Carol asked.

"What, the U.P.?"

"Well yeah, that too, but I meant the bridge."

Scott considered for a moment. "Absolutely. Remember, a military plane once took on the Big Mac and lost. It's got to be sturdier and better constructed than the roads."

"That doesn't mean much," Carol replied.

"Not with Michigan roads, anyway," Scott laughed derisively. "But I still doubt anything's going to take her down."

"What about the wind?" Allison piped up.

"I guess that is Big Mac's Achilles' heel. Not much wind today, though," Scott said.

Morning's first rays of light gleamed off the suspension bridge and made the water far beneath it sparkle. They'd found a safer place to spend the previous night but had taken off early in their haste to leave the Lower Peninsula.

Scott still couldn't believe a trip that never took more than six hours – and that was with a few stops – had stretched out over multiple days. He used to criticize post-apocalyptic shows for showing a short journey turning into a major, lengthy excursion. Now he knew better.

"Dad, look! We can go!" Allison said with renewed optimism.

Snapping back to attention, he put the car in drive and inched closer to the bridge.

CHAPTER FIFTEEN

Fossil, OR

Everyone beamed at Crandall as they finished following him in a prayer.

"The time we've waited so long for is finally nigh," he said.

Tears streamed down the faces of the Devotees. Some of them lifted their arms toward the Heavens as if hoping to reach their reward even sooner.

A murmur ran through the nearby tree roots, and each tree's leaves quivered. *These fools will meet God today,* the sentient roots whispered, *but not the one they're expecting.*

A sharp wind blew through the hills, bringing with it the attention of every bird and animal on the expansive property. A Western screech owl made a rare daytime appearance and called out an invitation to any stragglers. *After all,* the owl thought, *no one's going to want to miss this.*

"Joel and Thomas have blessed us many times over with their hard labor, and so they will be the first to meet Him," Crandall declared.

Shock transformed their features, followed by the brightest smiles anyone in the group had ever witnessed.

"Are you sure?" Joel asked Crandall.

"Yes, my child," Crandall replied.

Joel and Thomas shared a quick look before bowing in their leader's direction. If not for Crandall, they knew neither of them would have been blessed at all.

"What do we do?" Thomas asked.

"Simply walk forward until you fall."

The slightest flicker of hesitation crossed Joel's face.

"Do not worry," Crandall cooed. "You will be lifted up by His embrace. But first, you must willingly throw yourself into the pit and ask Him to take you home."

Hesitant no more, Joel and Thomas agreed to fall into their respective holes together at the count of three.

"One," the entire group chanted. "Two. Three!"

Both men took two steps forward and fell. Crandall and his twelve remaining Devotees collectively held their breath for a beat before breaking into a rousing round of applause.

Heartrending screams halted the revelry. Confused, Devotees called out, "What's happening?" "Where are they?" "Why aren't they being lifted?"

Crandall's resolve faltered, but he regrouped quickly. "Now, now, my children. We can't question the Lord's actions or His intent. We know that we, the Devotees, have been called for this. A test is necessary, and we're all being tested right now. Hold firm with your faith. Don't fail Him!"

A woman's soft voice bucked up everyone's courage with the first few lines of *Amazing Grace*. They all joined in for the second verse.

"T'was Grace that taught my heart to fear
And Grace, my fears relieved
How precious did that grace appear
The hour I first believed."

With their spirits buoyed, the entire group took a step closer to their own freshly dug pits. If any of them were afraid of the seemingly endless drop before them, they kept it to themselves, perhaps singing even louder to drown out their concerns.

"Through many dangers, toils, and snares
We have already come
T'was grace that brought us safe thus far
And Grace will lead us home."

Blood rained upward from Joel and Thomas' pits. Voices cracked as fear grabbed their minds again. A few of the most faithful stopped in their tracks, while others stepped away from the edge.

"What is this?" one Devotee demanded.

"Yeah, what *is* this?" others echoed.

"You've led us astray!" a man accused Crandall with a pointing finger.

"No, he'd *never* do that!" another argued.

Emboldened by the confusion, roots slithered out of each pit. Their knobby wooden flesh twisted and turned across the ground.

"Oh my God," the first woman to start singing screamed, capturing a lot of attention for her blasphemy. "Look at the ground," she urged. "Run!"

Her feet moved first, but every other pair aside from Crandall's quickly followed. "Where are you going?" he demanded. "The Lord will forsake you!"

A few pairs of feet faltered, unsure whether to heed Crandall's warning or to abandon him altogether. Several Devotees lost their balance and were ripped to the ground as roots wrapped around their ankles. They fought for purchase with their hands and feet, but the unrelenting ground gave them no hand or footholds. Screams filled the valley as the roots broke ankle and leg bones with ease.

"Save me!" the first to have fled called out toward Crandall, who stood by in shock. *How could this be happening?* he asked the Lord before the truth crashed down on his shoulders.

Crandall had played this game for so long he'd truly convinced himself of his own lies. The Devotees were originally nothing more than a way to make some money and gain power over those he viewed as foolish. At what point had his game turned into a personal conviction? When had he decided to actually jump into the pits with them instead of covering the makeshift graves and taking each member's life savings with him?

All of Crandall's questions ceased to matter as the thickest, gnarliest-looking root on the property wrapped around his legs and tugged. Much like his entire flock, Crandall couldn't free himself from his fate. He could have sworn he heard laughter and applause while being sucked down a pit that would never deliver him to his Lord.

CHAPTER SIXTEEN

MacArthur, WV

"What the hell are you doing?" a nurse shrieked.

A hard-faced man with a sharp crewcut attempted to push past her, but the nurse forcibly stood her ground. He pointed his automatic rifle at her stomach, yet she still refused to yield.

"Listen, lady. If you don't get out of my way, I'm going to shoot you."

"I'll move after you explain yourselves," she said with grim determination.

"Fine," he huffed. "Have you even looked outside? The sick are everywhere. Animals keep attacking us. So, we're putting an end to all of it!"

"On whose orders?" she asked.

"The President's. Now get the fuck out of the way before I end you, too."

She wanted to protect her patients, but one glance at the other nearby soldiers told her any efforts would be fruitless. *I need to survive so I can tell the world what they've done,* she thought. The nurse acquiesced, and the soldiers flooded past her. Gunfire echoed through the halls as diseased patients fell into the rapidly rising river of blood and bile. Tears streaked down the nurse's cheeks.

Rachel's body rebelled against her wishes. She urged her catatonic limbs to send her to the ground, but the hard chairs beneath her dwindling frame held on to her like a straightjacket. The nearly constant sound of rapid-fire bullets ripped her mind into two pieces; one, almost content to just let it happen, and the other, determined not to die.

The fight or flight signal running from her brain to her body finally kicked her limbs into gear. Rachel stumbled to the ground, falling face first into the muck. Revulsed, she turned her head and spat some of the rancid liquid from her mouth. Pushing the reality of what she'd almost just swallowed from her mind, she crawled forward at a pace any snail could have beaten.

Rachel dropped her head back into the river of bodily fluids as soldiers marched into the waiting room. Their guns erupted across the room in a back and forth manner, hitting everyone but her. She bit the inside of her cheek to keep from crying out when one industrious soldier kicked her in the ribs.

"Is that one still alive?" the lieutenant colonel called out.

"I don't think so," her assailant responded.

"You don't think so? Or you know so?"

The soldier hesitated for a second. Rachel was certain he could hear the rapid beating of her heart.

"I'm sure," the soldier finally said, turning heel and walking out of the room. The footsteps of several other soldiers followed his down the hall.

Rachel waited a few seconds before lifting her head imperceptibly above the reddish-black flood covering the floor. *I've got to get out of here.*

A single crack issued from behind her. Before she could react, her skull split open and brain tissue spattered against the wall. Rachel's head flopped back down, never to rise again.

That's why you've got to be absolutely sure, dammit, the lieutenant colonel thought while shaking his head in disgust.

CHAPTER SEVENTEEN

Cross Lanes, WV

A shudder rippled through Ivy's body. She's gasped, then shouted, "Stop! We have to turn around."

Thad's eyes widened. "We can't, Ivy," he motioning around at the chaos outside his truck. Traffic was barely moving, and they'd already seen half a dozen people walking down the highway die from brutal animal attacks.

"We can, and we must," Ivy insisted. "If you're not willing to do it, let me drive."

The raw exasperation in her tone caught his attention, as did the mournful quality beneath it. He considered his options for a second before cutting the wheel hard. Their heads bounced up and down as the vehicle's battered shocks took the impact of their improvised turnaround.

Thad wanted to ask questions, yet he held his tongue. The only thing he needed to know for sure right now was plastered all over Ivy's face. Something terrible had happened, and they needed to return to the hospital. The rational part of his brain tutted at him for going along with Ivy's apparent telepathy, but he knew even science couldn't explain the mental and emotional connection between twins.

"Hold on," Thad said as the road ahead became rougher. This side of I-64 stood almost vacant. Everyone had apparently intuited that heading north was the best way to survive.

Less than thirty minutes later, Thad brought the truck to a halt again. "Are you seeing this?" he asked, hopeful that the sight before him was a mirage.

"I'm seeing it," Ivy gritted her teeth. "And they're not going to stop us."

The finality in her tone shook all the doubt from Thad's mind. He would get her back to the hospital, no matter what it took. This madness had stolen his family, but that didn't mean it had to steal Ivy's family, too.

Thad revved the engine a few times in a futile attempt to scare off the crowd ahead. When they rushed forward instead of backing off, Thad threw the truck in drive and screeched toward the oncoming horde of sick people.

The mephitic stench of the crowd invaded the truck's cab, along with the unearthly groans escaping their tattered lips. Even at a distance, it was clear that none of these people were in their right minds. Aggressiveness had taken over, much like it had with the deer that'd started Thad, Ivy, and Rachel's entire misadventure.

Jesus, Thad thought. *They almost look like zombies.*

Thad double-checked his seatbelt mere seconds before the first wave of crazed ill people slammed to the ground underneath the truck's front grill. He didn't get a good look at any of them, but he could have sworn they all had various bite marks covering their bodies. The look in their eyes couldn't be mistaken, either. They had a fever that had driven out all reason and all hope. Only a shell of their former lives remained, and even that got snuffed out as their skulls crunched beneath the truck's tires.

Thad's stomach lurched with each crunch. Tears welled in his eyes as he contemplated all the lives he'd just ended. *What have I done? I'm a murderer.*

The truck rolled to a stop. Thad sat there, swallowed by his guilt and fear.

"Thad?" Ivy said. "We have to go."

He didn't reply.

"Thad! You need to hear me right now. We *have* to go! There are more of them, and they're not going to stop coming for us."

His trembling hands and vacant stare gave Ivy a single second of remorse for what she'd asked him to do.

"Move over," she barked. "I'm not going to let either of us die here."

She managed to push him out of the way and get herself belted in behind the wheel. A heartbeat later, she pushed the pedal all the way to the floor and skirted around another group headed their way.

The sick men and women reached out toward the truck, but their arms were way too short to grab on to anything. Ivy was glad she avoided killing anyone, but she knew her luck might not hold for much longer.

Whatever it takes, she thought. *I'm coming, Rachel.*

CHAPTER EIGHTEEN

Grand Island, NY

Doreen's chest tightened as they crossed into Buckhorn Island State Park. Sure, they were staying on I-190 rather than wandering off into the wilderness, but she'd seen more than enough to be terrified of wildlife.

Jill urged the truck to drive faster. This section of the highway was surprisingly empty, but that didn't assuage her fears. If anything, it made her even more suspicious of what was ahead. She couldn't stop envisioning the organized attack the crows had launched against Don. The sound of his screaming would never leave her mind, and she questioned all of her decisions to date. Was she leading them into a trap?

Heavy air hung between the two women. They'd had normal relationship fluctuations during their life together just like everyone else. But this felt different. They both wondered if they'd be able to recover, assuming they could survive long enough to get to the next border crossing.

An eerie silence loomed outside the truck. It was as if every creature in the nearby woods had entered into a very competitive game of freeze tag, and none of them were willing to move first.

"Jill?" Doreen whispered.

"Yes?"

"I love you," Doreen said.

Jill closed her eyes for a second and released a deep sigh. She squeezed her wife's hand. "I love you, too."

Awkward silence fell over the truck once again, but their spirits had lifted with the simple act of reaffirming their love for one another. They'd faced more than their fair share of troublesome incidents throughout the years, but none of them had torn them apart. Neither would this, they silently vowed.

"What the..." Doreen shrieked as lightning fast blurs attacked her side of the truck. The vehicle rocked back and forth under the impact of countless bodies.

"Hold on," Jill yelled while struggling with the steering wheel.

A light-colored blur flew across the hood, and Jill's eyes bulged. *That's not a crow.* Panic seized the back of her mind, but she fought it just like she'd been taught during her nursing program.

Dozens of bodies collided again and again with the truck, not seeming to care when bones snapped. Coyote growls took precedence over whimpers.

Jill coaxed the wheels forward a few more feet before a massive burst of energy flipped the truck and sent it rolling into a ravine. Branches punched through the windshield, spraying the women with shards of glass. Gravity seemingly abandoned them as their bodies flung in multiple directions. Seatbelts strained to the breaking point, and neither woman could tell the difference between their own yells of terror and their wife's.

CHAPTER NINETEEN

Mackinaw City, MI

The Mackinac Bridge held up the weight of way too many cars – plus a few pedestrians – without complaining. The deck sat 200 feet above Lake Michigan, with the towers piercing the clouds several hundred feet higher.

Allison and Carol eyed the bridge wearily, but Scott finally began to relax. He'd almost completed his primary task – to deliver his family safely to the Upper Peninsula. And just in time, too, as the shaking in his hands had almost reached the point where he'd have no choice but to drink or ride out the withdrawal symptoms.

On the other side, he promised himself before unconsciously patting the tiny alcohol bottle in his pocket. They'd inched across the halfway mark a few minutes ago, and he'd impulsively decided to kiss the ground once they reached the other side.

A light rumbling shook the car's undercarriage, followed by their feet.

"What's that?" Allison asked.

"What?" Scott asked, although he knew what she meant.

"I'm sure it's nothing, sweetie," Carol said.

Just a little farther, Scott thought as he sat on his left hand to hide its tremors. Sweat dotted his forehead and upper lip.

"Are you okay?" Carol asked.

"Huh?" he looked toward her. "Oh…yeah, I'm fine. No worries," he managed to grin.

Carol understood and battled her conflicted feelings. Of course, he'd have to go through withdrawal to get truly clean. But now? Why the hell did he have to drink in the first place? They needed him now more than ever, but he looked like a faded, wrung out shirt tossed on the side of the road. Would he even make it the U.P. before his entire body became gripped by tremors?

"Wait," Carol said. "Did you feel that?"

"Yes, Mommy," Allison said.

"What?" Scott replied.

"You really didn't notice that?" Carol asked. "The whole bridge shook."

"Oh," he said. *Maybe it's not me?*

An ear-splitting boom ripped every thought from their minds. Scott checked himself, followed by his family. Everyone looked okay. A glance around the bridge returned the same assessment. So, what the hell had just happened?

"Daddy," Allison's voice shook.

"What is it, sugar?" he asked.

She pointed a shaking finger at the sky to the northwest.

Scott and Carol sucked in a breath as the entire sky filled with a noxious, pitch-black smoke. *Shit,* they thought simultaneously.

"Forest fire?" Carol suggested.

"Most likely," Scott agreed. "Okay, listen up. This doesn't change anything. We'll just drive around it, okay? We can't expect anywhere to be perfect, right?"

His wife and daughter nodded, but he knew they were every bit as disheartened as he was. Had they made this trip for nothing?

Stuck again in standstill traffic, Scott's mind wandered back to his secret bottle. It had gone from bright to darkness so fast. He could barely make out his wife's frame. Would anyone notice if he took a little nip? Before he could decide, a chorus of honking horns broke his concentration.

"What the fuck?" Scott mumbled.

"Dad!" Allison chided him for swearing.

"Sorry." He didn't notice his lips moving as the latest threat made itself clear. The vehicles at the end of the bridge were trying to turn around. *Where do they think they're going to go?*

Golden-red light pierced through the darkness, accompanied by the distinct aroma of a bonfire. The drivers behind him had no illusions about being able to turn around. They jammed their cars into reverse instead.

Scott tried to discern what the threat was when the minivan ahead of him backed into the family car's front bumper. Scott waved his arms and yelled, "What the hell, man?"

"Scott," Carol said. He either ignored her or couldn't hear her outrage. His arms continued to flail and angry words peppered the air.

"Scott!" Carol grabbed his arm. "Stop it!"

He looked at her in shock.

"What?" he asked in an exasperated tone.

"You have to reverse out of here, Scott."

"I don't…"

"Dammit, Scott. For once in your life, just listen to me! Put this car in reverse right fucking now!"

Befuddled by her command, he slipped the car into reverse and let it ease backward.

CHAPTER TWENTY

MacArthur, WV

Ivy stood outside the hastily erected gate that blocked off the entire hospital. A soldier pointed his gun at her chest.

"I need you to turn around, get back in your truck, and leave right now," he said.

"My sister is here. I need to see her," she begged.

"Staff or patient?" he barked.

"Patient."

"She's not here anymore, then."

"What?"

"They were all ex...evacuated," he said. A slight hint of redness colored his cheeks. If the lieutenant colonel had heard him stumble like that...

"I don't understand. She was here only a few hours ago," Ivy countered.

"And I'm telling you she's not here now."

"Where is she, then? And where did the police go?" Tears of frustration silently rolled down Ivy's cheeks.

"That's classified," the soldier said without even a hint of compassion.

"I don't believe you," she spat. "I *know* something's wrong with my sister. Let me in, dammit!"

The soldier laughed. "Of course, there's something wrong with her. There's something wrong with all of them. Now listen closely because I'm not going to say this again. She's. Not. Here. They were evacuated and put into quarantine. You'll be contacted when she's better. But for now, you need to leave."

Ivy could see the lie in the soldier's eyes. The way he held his gun wasn't a lie, though. She slumped back into the truck.

Thad eyed her carefully. He'd barely begun to recover from the trauma of running sick people over.

"So... I guess that's that, then?" Thad asked.

Ivy turned the truck around and drove back down the neighborhood street. Approaching from the back hadn't worked this time. Maybe she needed to try a more direct approach.

Saying nothing, Ivy drove to the front gate, which blocked half of the parking lot. "This doesn't make any sense," she said aloud to herself.

Ivy squinted her eyes, trying to get a better look at the hospital. All the lights were off, but that wasn't surprising. The absolute absence of noise concerned her way more than anything else. Perhaps the soldier had told the truth? But then why did her gut scream that her sister was not only inside but in trouble?

Unwilling to risk another altercation with a trigger-happy soldier, she pulled out of the lot and parked half a block away. Time passed slowly, and even the vigilance behind her bad feeling couldn't keep sleep at bay. Her eyes snapped shut, and both of them tumbled into bad dreams.

CHAPTER TWENTY-ONE

Buckhorn Island State Park, NY

Jill and Doreen hung upside down. Jill couldn't figure out why, until she'd revived enough to remember the accident. Her fingers ached as she depressed the seatbelt button and braced for impact.

"Doreen? Can you hear me? Wake up, Doreen!"

Panic returned, and it took all of Jill's training for her to avoid breaking down. Blood leaked from Doreen's forehead. The gash looked deep and would leave a scar. *If she survives,* Jill thought.

Jill ripped off the bottom half of her shirt and wrapped it around the wound. She knew Doreen couldn't stay suspended upside down for much longer. All her wife's blood was steadily rushing into her face, which caused the wound to bleed much more than usual.

Preparing herself to catch Doreen, Jill contorted her body painfully and depressed the seatbelt. Doreen dropped, and Jill struggled to flip her over. "Okay, lady. I need you to hold on now, do you hear me? Don't you dare die on me. We're not done yet," Jill cried.

She knew she had the necessary training to help Doreen, but the sheer amount of blood pooled in the truck's cab made her question if any amount of training would be enough. It's not like she could open one of her veins and start a transfusion. There were no supplies, and she wasn't the right blood type. Yet she couldn't exactly carry Doreen out of the woods, either.

"Damn you, Don!" she yelled. Jill's voice echoed harshly around the cab, but Doreen's eyelids didn't even flutter.

I'm going to lose her, Jill realized. Sobs wracked her bruised and battered body. *This was all for nothing.*

A few trees away, a small group of crow scouts watched Jill's grief. Those that had lost loved ones during the truck attack felt vindicated. Others sat with a mixture of apathy and compassion. None did anything to further help or hinder the women's odds of survival.

CHAPTER TWENTY-TWO

Mackinaw City, MI

Fiery embers floated through the air. Thick, sulfurous smoke coated Scott's lungs. He gasped for fresh air, but his head swam with his latest inhalation of carbon dioxide. Drivers all around him panicked, crashing their cars into the sides of the bridge. The vehicle directly behind him sat empty, its wide-open doors evidence of a hasty retreat.

"Time to bail," he croaked out, and his family flew free of the ash-covered car. Scott picked up Allison, shared a quick glance with his wife, and they both started running.

Weaving in and out of the abandoned vehicles was much harder than Scott had anticipated. Allison slipped from his grasp, but he caught her before she hit the ground.

"Daddy!" she squealed.

"I'm sorry, sweetie," he said. Soot and irritation sent burning tears down his face.

"Daddy!" Allison insisted. "What's that?" She pointed behind him with a wild expression of terror he'd never seen before.

Afraid to look and even more terrified not to, he carefully spun his head. *That's impossible,* his mind protested. *That quite simply can't happen. Not here.*

The battle between rationalism and reality stuck his feet to the concrete for a moment. Scott's mouth hung open as the impossible surged ever closer. A shriek cut through his disbelief, issued by a woman running out of the black smoke. Her hair and clothing were ablaze. Her charred skin blistered black, and a wave of molten lava nipped at her heels.

Startled back to reality, Scott's feet pounded the ground until he caught up with his wife. The lava flow continued to speed up, and the couple knew they wouldn't make it off the bridge in time.

"What do we do?" Carol asked, eyeing the only possible solution.

"We jump," Scott confirmed.

"Won't that kill us?"

"Not any worse than that will," Scott nodded toward the lava.

Carol's vision skittered around the immediate area before falling on a large road sign laying on the ground. She hefted it, determined to put something between herself and the water 200 feet below.

"Allison?" Carol called.

"I've got her," Scott said.

"Save her, Scott. Nothing else matters."

The thinnest stream of lava melted the bottom of Scott's shoes as he helped his wife and child pivot over the barrier. He managed to hand Carol the road sign before leaping over without a second to spare.

"I love you both," Scott said, followed by, "Jump!"

Their bodies soared downward. Scott held his daughter to his chest while falling backward. He issued a silent prayer, then collided with Lake Michigan.

CHAPTER TWENTY-TWO

MacArthur, WV

Ivy jolted awake. Soldiers and Army vehicles rushed past, and she instinctively sunk down into the driver's seat. "Get down!" she hissed at a barely conscious Thad, who followed her directions without any questions.

When the sound of the troops evacuating settled down, she dared to peak her head above the steering wheel. The surrounding area sat as empty as a ghost town. Ivy stepped out of the truck, stretched toward the sky, and began walking back to the hospital.

Thad rushed to catch up. "What are we doing?" he asked.

"Checking out the hospital. I still don't believe them."

"Hang on," he said.

She shot him a deadly stare and he raised his hands. "I don't mean don't go. Just hold on for a sec. I've got a flashlight back in the truck."

Her impatience made it difficult to wait, but she managed to hold on long enough for Thad to jog back to her side.

"Here," he said, handing her their sole source of illumination.

Certain it would be locked, she reached for the gate's handle. "Oh!" she blurted as the handle granted them easy entry. Did this confirm the soldier's story? Or were they simply in too much of a hurry to do their jobs?

Ivy and Thad strode up to the building. She noted that sleeping seemed to have restored his nerve and was grateful for it. The front door to the hospital sat wide open, as if inviting them in.

"What if it's a trap?" Thad whispered.

"Well, I guess we'll find out soon enough," Ivy said.

The sharp, coppery tang of blood hit their noses. A second scent assaulted them, making their eyes water and their lungs rebel. "Holy shit," Thad managed to eke out between coughs.

Ivy's grim visage twisted with sorrow and fear. A smell this horrible could only mean one thing, right? Pulling the top of her shirt over her nose, she clicked on the flashlight and stepped onto the sticky, blood-soaked hospital floor.

The light paled in comparison to the inky darkness, but it pierced the oppressive, interior midnight well enough for the duo to see bodies lying everywhere.

Ivy shook as the flashlight highlighted the cause of death: Gunfire. "No. No. No!" Rage and grief overwhelmed her senses and she tumbled toward the ground. Thad caught her before she fell into the macabre flood that almost covered their feet.

She pressed her face into his chest, sobbing and bashing her fists against his shoulders. Thad held on tightly, undeterred by her violent outburst.

"How could they do this?" she asked with the bewildered tone of a young child.

"I don't know," Thad said. "But we should go before they come back."

"I'm not leaving without her."

Fear soaked his mind. He didn't want to die. But he didn't want her to be alone, either. Unable to speak for fear of showing his cowardice, he nodded and took her hand.

They navigated up the dark staircase and the gore-filled hallways while trying not to look too closely at the dead. The stench overpowered them several times, forcing them to dry-heave. By the time Rachel's broken body laid at their feet, Ivy's will to live had vacated the premises.

"Okay, help me lift her up," Thad encouraged her.

"I-I'm gonna stay here instead. Sorry, Thad."

"The hell you are! If you stay here, you'll die. Do you think that's what Rachel would want for you? Let's get her – and ourselves – out of here!"

Sighing, Ivy allowed herself to be led by Thad. *Maybe he has a point,* she pondered. This was far from the first time she'd felt destroyed by life, but she'd always bounced back. She had to do this for her sister. Rachel deserved a real resting place. More importantly, she deserved justice.

Ivy clung to her sister's legs with renewed purpose as they made their way downstairs. She would take on the entire government if necessary. Someone would pay for killing her sister.

The exit loomed ahead, and she found herself already working on a tell-all blog post. *If the power ever comes back, that is...*

Ivy's thoughts were interrupted by an odd beeping sound that quickly filled the entire hospital. "What *is* that?" she yelled, forcing herself not to drop her sister's legs, despite the overwhelming urge to plug her ears.

"I don't kn..." Thad began before the entire world disappeared.

CHAPTER TWENTY-THREE

Mackinaw City, MI

Scott's back flopped against Lake Michigan like it had hit a force shield. The snapping of his tailbone rung out in sync with the tiny bottle shattering in his pocket. Glass embedded itself in his leg and groin, followed by the pulverizing impact of his elbows against the tense surface. Somehow, he held on to the small girl shrieking in his arms, thereby protecting her from the worst of the blunt force trauma.

"Swim hard, Allison. Swim, and don't look back," he had shouted a few seconds before impact. Stunned by the harshness of the water, she almost sunk too far beneath the surface before heeding her father's last words. Righting herself, she paddled with all her strength against the lake's mighty current as the lake claimed her father's shattered body.

Allison put everything she had into reaching her goal, but her energy lagged quickly. The land looked no closer after ten minutes, and she sobbed with the fear of death. *It's too far. I can't.*

Allison's forward movement slowed, and her thin limbs threatened to stop. Her head bobbed up and down beneath the surface. Exhausted and terrified, she cried out for her dad, unaware he could no longer help.

"Allison? Is that you? Hold on, baby girl!"

The most wonderful sound the young girl had ever heard! Or was it nothing more than a hallucination? She did her best to tread water in a circle, hoping against hope that she'd spot her mom.

"I've got you," Carol said.

"Mommy," Allison cried. "I can't find Dad. I think he's dead." Convulsions shook Allison's shoulders.

Silent tears streaked down Carol's face for a few seconds before she ordered herself to stop. "I'm sorry, sweetie," Carol said gently while pulling her daughter up onto the road sign that had helped break her fall. Dropping off to the side, Carol adopted a determined countenance. *I can do this.* She pushed the sign and slowly swam with three limbs.

CHAPTER TWENTY-FOUR

Buckhorn Island State Park, NY

Pink and orange hues painted the sky as the sun began its evening descent. Doreen hadn't shown any signs of regaining consciousness, but the bleeding had stopped and she was still breathing. With the front area of the truck unsuitable as a shelter, Jill had placed her wife on a crudely constructed sled made from nearby materials.

The two now rested beneath the upside-down truck bed. As far as shelters went, it definitely could have been worse. Crackling sounds emitted from the fire Jill had built a few feet away from the vehicle. She'd also managed to gather a few useful supplies from the front seat, including a thin blanket.

Jill's parched lips and rumbling stomach made it clear she needed to find food and water. But she couldn't stand the idea of leaving Doreen alone in the dark, so she'd decided to wait until daybreak to set off on an expedition.

Every noise turned her heart into a jackhammer. Oddly, though, the nocturnal denizens of the woods didn't attack. *Maybe our luck is finally changing,* Jill laughed bitterly to herself. With sleep evading her, she spent the night trying to keep her wife as warm as possible.

CHAPTER TWENTY-FIVE

MacArthur, WV

Disoriented, Thad thought the ringing in his ears came from a telephone. "W-what the f-fuck?" he mumbled. A sharp cough burst free of his dust-coated lungs. He experimented with his fingers and toes. They all seemed to respond to his non-verbal commands. He turned his neck and spotted a desk hovering haphazardly over his head.

"Ivy?" he rasped.

Only settling debris pierced the eerie silence.

He cleared his throat and tried again. "Ivy?"

Crawling out of his hidey-hole, he was stunned to see the damage around him. *Wait. How can I see anything? The power is out.* He rubbed the grit from his eyes and tried to orient himself. Thad's stomach dropped as an upward glance revealed nothing but smoke and barely visible stars. The thick molasses of his battered mind began putting the pieces together.

They blew it up? That beeping...it must have been the final countdown. And that means...

"Ivy! Ivy, where are you?"

He sorted through the rubble, tossing aside broken bricks, wood, and hospital equipment. *They can't be far.* His frantic search continued for several minutes until he spotted her hair.

"Oh shit, Ivy." Thad threw the remaining barriers aside until her beautiful face – now crumpled almost beyond recognition – lifelessly stared past him. *Please, no. Let it be Rachel. Let it be Rachel!* he silently begged the Heavens.

More debris flew through the air until a shirt became visible. Thad fell to his knees and pounded the ground. *Not you, too,* he cried. *Why? Why did they do this? I'll kill them all,* he pledged, despite knowing he never would.

Memories of their brief time together flitted through his mind, along with a few scenes of the future he'd dared to dream. But how could such beautiful dreams possibly come true in such an ugly world?

"I'll make this right for you, Ivy. I'll finish what you started."

He kissed her grimy forehead, picked up her broken frame, and carried her to his truck. He gently placed her across the back seat where her sister had lain less than a day ago.

Leaving her felt wrong, but he had to fulfill her final wish. Thad reentered the remains of the VA hospital and searched anew until Rachel's twisted body came free of the debris. He laid her next to Ivy, placed their hands together, and allowed himself to break down behind the wheel.

His resolve returned after he shed tears for Ivy and the life they might have lived together. He'd also mourned for the death of Rachel, his parents, and the world as he'd once known it.

"I'm going to find a safe place for you now, ladies. I'm sorry I couldn't save you."

Thad drove off in search of a quiet, undestroyed area where he could give the twin sisters a peaceful final resting place.

CHAPTER TWENTY-SIX

One Week Later

Jill jabbed a large, pointed stick in the direction of a man who'd wandered into the makeshift camp.

"Whoa!" the man said before holding his hands up in a gesture of peace. "Let's not do anything too hasty, all right?"

She eyed him with great suspicion, especially his tattered park ranger uniform. "What are you doing here?" she barked.

"I'm here to help. I've been looking for survivors."

"To take them where, exactly?"

"How long have you been here?" he asked.

"Long enough. You're the first person I've seen in days."

"So, you don't know that it's over, then," he gave her a tentative smile.

"What do you mean, it's over?"

"Whatever it was – and man, some of the theories are a real doozy – it all just stopped. No more sinkholes, fires, or animal attacks. It's almost like it never even happened. Well, aside from all the damage and dead people."

"For real?" Jill's voice shook.

"Absolutely, ma'am."

"Do you have a vehicle?"

"Yeah, about a quarter mile from here."

"Please, help me. She needs medical attention." Jill rushed to the shelter and began slowly pulling Doreen out.

"Holy shit! Is she still alive?" he asked.

"Yes, but just barely, and not for much longer. It's a miracle she made it this far. Now please, help me," Jill implored with tears in her eyes.

"She's going to be okay, ma'am."

The park ranger radioed the closest triage center before running for his truck.

CHAPTER TWENTY-SEVEN

Two Weeks Later

"It's been almost two weeks since the last incident. Sinkholes, unexplained fires, and so-called extinct volcanoes erupted worldwide, including one in Michigan's Upper Peninsula that had lain dormant for billions of years.

"Authorities are still unsure what caused all of these natural disasters, although experts in various fields theorize that it was a rapid extinction event, perhaps caused by the earth itself. Of course, naysayers across the globe have spoken out loudly against any of this being the result of man-made climate change."

Carol tried not to roll her eyes. After everything they'd been through, how could anyone believe that the planet and all of its wildlife hadn't ganged up against the human race? She let the hand-crank radio die and returned to stroking her daughter's hair.

"I miss Dad," Allison said.

"I do, too, sweetie. I do, too." Carol was surprised to discover she truly meant it.

Her thoughts drifted back to that day in Lake Michigan. She'd pushed herself so hard and so far, only to be greeted by the sight of lava spreading across her destination. Heartbroken, she'd considered giving up. If it hadn't been for Allison, she probably would have. Unsure what else to do, she treaded water for more than an hour, praying for someone to rescue them.

A red and white ship piloted by the Canadian Coast Guard eventually answered her prayers. Crewmembers pulled Carol, Allison, and a few other survivors on board before ferrying them all the way to Manitoulin Island. They'd spent a few days at Mindemoya Hospital before being put up at a local hotel.

No one knew how it happened, but more than a third of the world's population died within one week. And now, everything had somehow already begun returning to normal. But as much as she'd always loved nature, Carol knew she'd never be able to stop side-eyeing animals and trees. People would rebuild the destroyed roads and buildings, of course, but she couldn't help wondering if they should.

CHAPTER TWENTY-EIGHT

"How's she doing?"

"They say she's going to make it, Jake. Thanks to you." Jill flung her arms around the park ranger and kissed his cheek. "You saved her. You saved both of us. Thank you."

He grew a bit uncomfortable with the woman's gratitude and shifted the red baseball cap on his head. "It wasn't anything anyone else wouldn't have done."

Jill eyed the hat and remembered how much she'd hated it sitting on top of Don's judgmental head. "You'd be surprised," she said. *And so am I,* she marveled at the difference between the two men with seemingly similar views. *Maybe there's hope for all of us yet.*

The trees outside whispered and plotted. They knew they would be unleashed again the next time the human population surged past the breaking point. They gleefully counted down to mankind's next extinction event.

AUTHOR'S NOTE

Thank you for reading *Sinkhole: A Horror Story.* I hope you enjoyed reading it as much as I did writing it. If so, please share this story with your horror-loving friends and consider posting a review to Amazon and/or Goodreads. It would be greatly appreciated!

SPOILER ALERT: If you haven't read the book yet, please skip the rest of this note until after you reach the story's conclusion.

The inspiration for this book came from two sources: a series of natural disasters and a news story about overpopulation. It may be a contentious subject for some, but the planet is currently showcasing the deleterious effects of global climate change. Some scientists have gone so far as to warn us that life as we know it will cease to exist by 2050 unless drastic measures are taken immediately.

With all of this in mind, I wondered what would happen if the planet decided that it was time for a partial extinction event that would dramatically cut the human population. In most man vs. nature stories, the planet – and all of nature – is not actually taking a side against us. Instead, it acts without bias and without a grudge. The deadly action within these stories is horrifying, but there's never a sense that the planet could stop the downfall of humanity if it merely wanted to.

In *Sinkhole,* the planet is fully in control of everything that befalls humanity. Although much of the work is carried out by its faithful denizens, the devastation could be brought to a stop with a single command. This makes the joyful glee that the participants of the massacre take in destroying a third of the human race even more horrific.

This horror is paralleled by the destructive, and self-destructive, nature of many of the book's characters. Some, like Don, would rather be destroyed than accept help from people they don't agree with. Others, like Crandall, think they have all the answers and will happily lead people to their deaths in order to prove their superiority.

The religious beliefs of these characters – and of the trees – did not bring about their downfall. That honor belongs solely to their extremism and inability to accept and respect the many differences that make the world an endlessly fascinating place to live. And ultimately, that's the point of *Sinkhole.* After all, if everyone could learn to work together for the good of all humanity, we might not have to live in fear of each other and the future of the planet.

Fact Checking

As always, I included a lot of real-life places, facts, and history in *Sinkhole*. For example, there really is an extinct volcano in Michigan's Upper Peninsula. I did move its location, though, for dramatic effect.

Dunns, WV, is also similar to the description provided, although I hear it's getting bigger and more modern each year. Dunns is where my mother and aunt where raised. The Meadors are part of my family line, and Rachel and Ivy are family names. I did take some liberty with the spelling of Ivy, though, which was originally Ivie.

Centralia, PA, is very real, as is the coal fire that's been burning underneath the town for decades. It was also the inspiration for the setting of the *Silent Hill* movie.

Get in Touch!

Do you have any questions or comments? You can contact me at www.aprilataylor.net or via social media:

facebook.com/aprilataylorhorror
twitter.com/aprilataylor
instagram.com/aprilataylorwriter/

Book Recommendations

I have greatly enjoyed and recommend the following recent and upcoming books for horror fans:

- Inspection by Josh Malerman
- The Deep by Alma Katsu
- Growing Things and Other Stories by Paul Tremblay
- Ghoster by Jason Arnopp
- The Twisted Ones by T. Kingfisher
- Here There Are Monsters by Amelinda Berube
- The Dead Girls Club by Damien Angelica Walters

ACKNOWLEDGEMENTS

Thank you to every reader who has taken the time to read and review my books. Your support means the world to me. Thank you also to everyone who has sent me an email or letter. I've been honored to read the personal stories that some of you have shared, and I'm proud that my books have touched you in some way.

Thank you to Anne for her continual support. I couldn't do this without you! Sorry I couldn't keep the original, more upbeat ending. Without that last paragraph, this book just wouldn't be me. Despite that, I'm so grateful to you for inspiring the message of hope that came just before the end.

Thank you to my beta readers, Christina, Tina, and Anne. Your comments always make my books better than they would have been otherwise.

Thank you to Greta Thunberg and everyone else who is fighting to make the world a better place for all of us.

Looking for a new story to read?

Be sure to check out my other books! Thank you for your support.

Corvo Hollows: A Psychological Thriller

The Haunting of Cabin Green: A Modern Gothic Horror Novel

Missing in Michigan: Alexa Bentley Paranormal Mysteries Book One

Frightened in France: Alexa Bentley Paranormal Mysteries Book Two

Lost in Louisiana: Alexa Bentley Paranormal Mysteries Book Three

Vasilisa the Terrible: A Baba Yaga Story (Midnight Myths and Fairy Tales #1)

Death Song of the Sea: A Celtic Story (Midnight Myths and Fairy Tales #2)

Made in the USA
Las Vegas, NV
25 April 2021